Ray Gonzalez

# The Ghost of John Wayne

## AND OTHER STORIES

THE UNIVERSITY OF ARIZONA PRESS   TUCSON

The University of Arizona Press
© 2001 Ray Gonzalez
First printing
All rights reserved
♾ This book is printed on acid-free, archival-quality paper.
Manufactured in the United States of America
06   05   04   03   02   01     6   5   4   3   2   1

Library of Congress Cataloging-in-Publication Data
Gonzalez, Ray.
The ghost of John Wayne, and other stories / Ray Gonzalez.
p. cm. — (Camino del sol)
ISBN 0-8165-2065-8 (cloth) —
ISBN 0-8165-2066-6 (pbk.)
1. Southwestern States—Social life and customs—
Fiction.   2. Mexican American Border Region—
Fiction.   3. Hispanic Americans—Fiction.   I. Title.
II. Series.
PS3557.O476 G48 2001
813'.54—dc21
2001001465

British Library Cataloguing-in-Publication Data
A catalogue record for this book is available from the British Library.

Publication of this book is made possible in part by the proceeds of a permanent endowment created with the assistance of a Challenge Grant from the National Endowment for the Humanities, a federal agency.

# CONTENTS

*Part One*

# THE SCORPION EATER

He held it up to the candlelight so Miguel could see it glowing in the jar. It twitched and twisted its tail, the flickering light moving through its body like pulses of danger. Miguel watched as the man drew the jar closer and removed the wire screen that served as a lid. The man, who had a black moustache and tied his hair back in a ponytail, nodded. Miguel wondered where his *abuela* had met such a strange person, but he did not ask him any questions, not even his name. He had no choice but to sit and watch the stranger play with the scorpion in the jar.

Miguel's parents were dead and his abuela was lost in the cantina, and this man came to visit him often. He told him he was a friend of his abuela. He usually brought Miguel a piece of fruit or a large bottle of soda, sometimes a whole plate of delicious *enchiladas* from the cantina. Miguel thought the man with the long hair worked in the cantina, a place where his abuela spent most of her time. Tonight was different because the stranger brought the large scorpion in the jar. He sat at the kitchen table and motioned to the boy to join him. At first, Miguel wanted to run when he saw what was in the jar, thinking this man might want to set the scorpion loose on him.

"Don't worry, Miguel," the man said. "Your abuela knows I am with you tonight. She told me to watch over you. She gave me this as a gift. This is her jar, and the scorpion belongs to her. She told me this is the kind of magic we have because she and I love each other. It is like the love she has for you. She is a good abuela. Don't ever forget that, Miguel."

Miguel didn't understand what the man was telling him. He knew his grandmother loved him, but he was tired of spending every night alone. The stranger's visits helped to take the loneliness away, but he was tired of him, not knowing what to think about his behavior and the unusual stories he told. As he watched him remove the screen from the top of the jar, Miguel realized the scorpion was not for him. It was a gift from his abuela to the man, one of her boyfriends, even though Miguel had not seen them together in her bedroom for a long time. The man tipped the jar and carefully brought it to his face. The scorpion slid to the bottom of the jar as he tilted it. It hit the bottom, then started to climb up the smooth glass. Miguel could see its pale red legs and its gnarled yellow tail stiff and alert. The tip of its stinger glistened black in the dimly lit room. The man did not tremble but held the jar steady in both hands. Miguel pushed his chair farther away and yearned for his abuela to come home.

He rose from the chair, trying not to startle the scorpion, and glanced toward the door, ready to run. His fascination with what the man was doing kept him from moving. Miguel thought of the last time he had found this man in bed with his abuela. They had blown out all the candles in the small house. Miguel was awakened by the sounds in his abuela's room. He lay still and heard the moans. He thought his abuela was hurt and tiptoed across the dark house to her room. When he reached the open door, this man was on top of his abuela. They didn't notice him, and their naked bodies kept moving in the dark. He watched for a few seconds until a shadow in the open window startled him and he went back to his room.

The man opened his mouth wide as the scorpion stopped a few inches from his steady lips. Miguel wanted to say something and stop the man from playing this kind of trick on him. Suddenly, the man tapped the jar hard against his open mouth, and the scorpion disappeared into it. Miguel covered his eyes with his hands and heard the man swallow with a large gulp. He moved his hands from his face to see the man drink from a bottle of beer. The man put it down with a thud and tapped the empty jar on the table with his fingers. He wiped his lips with the back of his right hand, his dark eyes reflecting the burning candle that flickered on the other end of the table. The man reached behind his head and loosened his long hair from its tie. He shook his head, and his hair cascaded over his shoulders.

"Are you okay?" Miguel asked.

The man nodded, rose from his chair, and grabbed the candle. Miguel followed him outside, the flame guiding the two of them into the black night. Miguel stood next to the stranger, hoping they had stepped outside to greet his abuela. He waited for the man to do something, but all he did was hold the candle and stare down the dark streets. Miguel thought he saw someone coming up the street, but the shadow vanished in the trees surrounding the adobe houses. With a jolt, the man grabbed his stomach, groaned loudly, and went back inside. Miguel followed and shut the door. The man sat at the table and did not move for a long time, then lay his head over his crossed arms. Miguel thought about the scorpion in the man's stomach, hoping his abuela would show up. He remembered the story she had recently told him about her brother Efren, who had been killed by a powerful tornado that had hit the town years before Miguel was born. She said Efren had been found high up in a tree. The force of the tornado had thrown him atop a giant cottonwood that had survived the heavy winds. People saw the tree hanging over the river and came running when someone said there was a body up there. His abuela was glad to find her brother because six other people had disappeared in the tornado. They brought him down and buried him near the river. She told Miguel the story to let him know their *pueblo* was a special place to live and Miguel should watch the sky and the river, paying attention to the huge cottonwoods that lined the water and that led to a bigger world she said Miguel would find someday.

Miguel wondered if the scorpion in the man's stomach was as strong as the tornado that had taken his abuela's brother into the sky. He waited and heard the man snoring at the table, then almost jumped out of his chair when his abuela entered. She burst through the door as if expecting to walk in on something terrible.

"What is he doing here?" his abuela demanded. Miguel could smell the cantina on her breath and clothes.

"He was staying with me like he always does. We were waiting for you to come home," Miguel said as his abuela tottered over him. "He told me you gave him the scorpion."

"What scorpion?" His abuela slapped Miguel on the head.

He sat down and tears streamed from his eyes. She shook the sleeping man. "¡Cabrón! Vámonos!" She tried to get him to leave.

When he wouldn't wake up, she pushed him off the chair. He fell loudly to the floor. Miguel couldn't tell which of the two was drunker but settled on his abuela. His abuela kicked the sleeping man.

"What's wrong with this *borracho*?" she asked.

"He ate the *alacrán*."

"What?" She turned threateningly toward Miguel.

"He ate the scorpion he said you gave him."

Her red eyes seemed to ignite as she realized what Miguel had been trying to tell her.

"Vámonos," she motioned to Miguel.

She grabbed him by the arm and dragged him out of the house. They moved quickly down the deserted street, the cool night air helping Miguel to fight off his terror. As she led him tightly by the hand, he turned to look at the house. His abuela had left the front door open. Miguel could see the candle still flickering. Its flame enlarged itself as it reached the bottom of the cup, and the light threw an arc across the open doorway. Right before they rounded the street corner, Miguel saw the silhouette of an enormous scorpion tail covering the glowing doorway. The last thing he saw was the quick way it struck and muffled the final seconds of the melting candle on the empty table.

# THE BLACK PIG

My grandmother Julia told me the black pig strolled into the village when she was fourteen years old and nobody could catch it. She said they had never seen it before but wondered how a black pig could enter the village without anyone claiming ownership of it. When several boys tried to catch it and tie it up, it ran down the dirt streets. It was a huge pig with scars all over its back, its sharp hooves a bright pink in contrast to its black body. My grandmother said the pig disappeared around the corner of one of the adobe houses and squeezed its bloated body under the wooden bridge that stood over the dry creek.

The boys surrounded the bridge but couldn't get the pig to come out. They poked it with sticks and threw rocks at it until Jose, my grandmother's brother, told them to leave the pig alone. The boys stopped and listened to the creature grunt and snort under the bridge. Some of them said it was stuck under there. Others knew that the behavior of pigs meant it was just hiding and could come out and attack them if it wanted. The pig waited and the boys waited. Nothing happened for a long time. Jose wanted the boys to go home and said he would coax the pig out and take it to his farm until somebody claimed it. My grandmother came down to the bridge after the boys gave up and left the pig alone. She watched Jose crawl under the bridge and heard him talking to the pig. The huge thing had calmed down, but my grandmother could hear an occasional oink as Jose tried to be friendly.

Suddenly, my grandmother heard a loud tearing noise as the wooden bridge shuddered and gave way. Jose tried to get out of the pig's path as it came charging out with half the bridge on its back, but he fell into the shallow creek bed. My grandmother said she had no choice but to jump in with him. The pig barely missed them as it churned up dust, wood, and mud while its swollen shape tried to climb to higher ground. With a loud squeal it made it over the top, shook off the last piece of wood, and ran toward the village. Jose and my grandmother reached the road just as the pig was chasing three boys down the street. She ran after it and waved to Jose to follow her. He hesitated, then caught up with her as they watched the pig squeeze under the fence of the corral that held Antonio Reyes's horses. The pig seemed at ease among the half dozen horses and settled down, though it made the horses nervous. They started to prance inside the corral. The pig lowered itself into a muddy corner and watched the horses grow more irritable with its presence. Jose opened the corral, carefully stepped in, and shut the gate behind him. He tried to calm the horses as Julia went to find Antonio. The pig rested on its swollen belly, ignoring Jose's slow approach. Julia found Antonio in his house, and they came running, a rope in Antonio's hands. Jose was ten yards from the quiet pig when Julia and Antonio's arrival forced its next move.

It waited for Antonio to swing the gate open and bounded faster than any pig should be able to move. It knocked Jose out of the way and followed three of the terrified horses that were galloping to freedom. Antonio managed to close the gate on the last three horses. My grandmother told me she had never seen such a sight as Jose flying through the air when the pig slammed into him and Antonio awkwardly attempting to keep the animals from fleeing through the gate. The pig bounded in the opposite direction from the loose horses as Antonio chased what belonged to him.

Jose shook the dirt off his clothes and ignored my grandmother's laughter when he came out of the corral. She pointed in the direction of the pig, but Jose had given up. He told Julia to forget about the crazy beast. Whoever owned it had to catch it. Julia followed Jose home and wondered what was going to happen to the mighty pig.

That night, my grandmother was falling asleep after having said her prayers. Jose was in the other room of their small adobe house. Their parents were asleep. She opened her eyes in darkness and looked toward the lone window in her room. A slight wind moved the curtains as she heard the cry of an animal in the darkness. She thought of the black pig, but this was not a pig sound. She had never heard anything like it before. She got dressed and went outside to find Jose standing on the front porch. He motioned to her to be quiet. They stared at the sliver of a moon in the clear night sky. They stood there, brother and sister, and listened to the strange cry. The nearest houses in the town were a hundred yards down the road, so my grandmother had no idea if other people could hear the animal cry.

Jose stepped into the front yard, where two giant cottonwoods towered over the house. The branches of the trees swayed in the wind, and she could hear the leaves ringing like tiny bells. The cry stopped as Jose reached the wooden gate at the front of their property. He leaned on it and looked up and down the dirt road. As Julia walked carefully to join him, she saw lights burning in some of the houses. They stood by the fence and waited. Earlier in the day, she had told their parents about the funny adventure with the pig. They had not said anything but had listened quietly to her account. She was surprised that her father had not come outside by now because he must have heard the sound, too.

She looked toward the porch. The pig stood quietly under one of the cottonwoods. She tapped her brother on the back and pointed. It was a dark night, but they could clearly make out the animal standing there, its head and deep eyes frozen in their direction. The moment Jose took a step forward—and my grandmother swears to this day it is true—she saw the area around the tree grow blacker and cover the spot where the pig stood. It was as if a blanket of darkness had been thrown over the animal, and not even the moonlight could penetrate the spot. The leaves in the tree shook as if a mighty storm had invaded them. My grandmother claims she and Jose couldn't move from where they stood. She felt a heavy weight grip her legs so they couldn't move. The cry that had brought them into the night sounded again as a shriek above the trees in the yard. Julia stared in amazement as the black mass rose swirling into the night air, bounced against the trunk of the tree, and carried itself away.

She said what happened next is the most vivid part in her memory. She recalls Jose's hair standing on end, as did hers. She wanted to cry out but couldn't speak or move her legs. Jose wanted to shout something but was mute. There was no wind, no storm, just the black mass that covered the pig, concealing its body from them as it rolled across their farm and disappeared beyond the cotton fields behind her family's house. They heard the distant cry once more. Then they were released, and the air was abruptly still. Brother and sister fell forward a couple of feet as the restraining force disappeared. They ran toward the house, but Jose told her not to yell out for their parents. He stopped under the tree and waved his sister over.

When my grandmother told me this story and got to this point, she stopped because tears came to her eyes. She reached for the purse she kept on her bedroom dresser and made sure her rosary was inside. She always carried one in her purse, though her age and bad health kept her from going anywhere. I had come to visit at her bedside when she told me this story. After reassuring herself by fingering the beads, she told me that her brother was standing over a burned spot on the ground. It was the exact place where she had last seen the pig. As she slowly drew nearer, she swears a strange look came upon Jose's face. She could see it in the darkness. She said her brother was never the same after that night.

The next day, they tried to convince their parents that they had not burned the grass in the yard. Her father was angry with them and insisted he had never heard any strange noises the previous night. He told them he had found out about the loose pig from some of the men in the village, but they told him it had disappeared and had probably been captured by the farmer who owned it. Jose did not tell his father about the incident under the tree. My grandmother said she couldn't tell her father what they had seen because he would think they had been drinking or doing evil things with other young people in the village.

My grandmother wept quietly as she finished the story. It had taken place seventy years before. Jose had disappeared twenty years ago to the day, she told me. It was common knowledge that my uncle was an alcoholic and a troublemaker. I was three years old when he left El Paso for good. My grandmother wiped her tears and admitted she was telling me something she had never told anyone else in my family. She always believed that the incident with the black pig had something to do with Jose's miserable life and disappearance. He grew older, went from odd job to odd job, then entered the army and was wounded in World War II. When he returned to El Paso, he became a senseless drunk. He was constantly getting into bar fights and winding up in jail, and he got two women pregnant.

When he left El Paso twenty years ago, Jose went to Albuquerque to stay with my aunt Maria. She put up with him for two months, then one day he disappeared. The Albuquerque police never found him, and the family has not heard from him since. No one knows if he is dead or alive. I knew about Jose vanishing, but the story of the black pig was new.

My grandmother quit crying as I prepared to end my visit. I said I would come back that weekend to buy some groceries for her at the neighborhood market. She asked me to promise I would not tell anybody in the family about the black pig until she was dead. I felt weird about her request but promised.

I recount this story three months after my grandmother's death. Two years have passed since she told me. I retell it because I have no idea what the encounter with the black pig meant or why it happened to my family. Why did my grandmother feel that Jose, a relative I never knew, was fated to live his kind of life because of the incident with the black pig? What about her? She also encountered the animal but lived a long and rich life. She raised a large family, though my grandfather, her husband, died forty years ago at a young age. I never knew him either. She lived to be ninety-six and was a strong, religious woman. What was it about the black pig that had made her share this story with me in her final years? Did she leave anything out? Can these things really have happened? I write this as I prepare to drive to northern New Mexico to visit the towns where my mother's family came from. One of these towns is the site of my great-grandfather's old farm. I don't know if it is still there. Located near Albuquerque, it has probably been paved over by the suburbs. I want to see where my grandmother grew up. As I get ready to go, I think about the black pig and wonder if the burned spot on the ground has anything to do with the difficult task of uncovering family secrets. Both sides of my family have hidden many things from me in their attempts to hold onto a past that has been scorched by powerful forces.

## CABEZA DE VACA

Cabeza de Vaca walks into the cave and finds the woman lying on a grass mat. Her sweating has soaked the blankets. It is dark in the cave, and a nearby fire has gone out. Some of the stones still glow, but Cabeza decides he doesn't need the light. She is only twenty feet from the entrance, which is blocked by a group of men who watch him closely. Cabeza kneels down, removes his bag from his shoulder, and examines the ill woman's naked body. She has a fever and doesn't know he is there, her eyes swollen shut, her arms stiff at her sides. Cabeza places a hand on her forehead and prays to the Lord that the warriors behind him do not kill him if he can't help her. This is the fourth sick member of the tribe he has seen. Two of the earlier ones recovered right away. When the third one died in his arms, the men dragged Cabeza away, stripped him, and tied him to crossed stakes. He stood, hung, and slept there for four days without food. They woke him by throwing water on him, and he licked the drops as they ran down his face. It was the only water he had for three more days until a woman whose body was painted in purple and orange brought him a gourd of water. She was naked under the paint, and Cabeza stared at her rippling chest as he drank. On the night of the fourth day his legs gave way and he hung from his arms, his bent knees almost touching the ground. He awoke in the morning sun and felt blue lizards climbing up his body. One of them bit him on the ear, and Cabeza shook his head. The lizards disappeared. Then he noticed a rattlesnake coiled a few feet away. It lay dazed in the hot sun. As Cabeza opened his eyes wider, someone threw water on him. He stood up, startled and gasping. Some of the water fell on the snake, so it struck and bit him on the right leg. He screamed and kicked it away. Before it could strike again, three arrows pinned the snake. Men came laughing and cut the wriggling snake into pieces. Cabeza was hurled backward in circles of yellow fire, the horizon lifting and dancing above the skirts of women who floated around him. Their long black skirts and white blouses told him he was back in Spain, the red clouds of naked men removing the garments from the women as they joined them in a dance no Spaniard knew. Cabeza was certain he was in Madrid, because the bulls had been proud and strong in the pen he visited with his father. He met Lourdes at the inn and they went upstairs. When his lover of four years started to remove her clothes, the wind picked up, and a dust storm covered the huts that surrounded him. The dust blew for several hours and pricked his floating body, one arm tied to the stake. The other, which had turned black, had long ago been cut off by his captors. The dust storm shrieked into the night. Cabeza counted the stars and heard the sound of running water at his feet. The next day they cut him down, carried him to a hut, and washed and fed him. He recovered in two days and was given back his few possessions before he was taken to the woman in the cave. Cabeza pulled a bag of herbs from his satchel and sprinkled them over the woman's sweating forehead. He took his rosary and started to pray. Cabeza swung his hands in the air above her body from head to foot. He repeated this several times, hoping for the best, then sat back and waited. He fell asleep against the cold wall. When he awoke, the woman was sitting next to him. Cabeza was instantly alert and stood up. She sat there, looking at him calmly. He turned to the entrance, which was clear. Not knowing what to do, he crept quietly to the opening and looked into the red explosion of the evening sun as it set across the western desert. As his eyes adjusted to the light, he jumped back when he saw the warriors lying dead outside the cave, dozens of arrows sticking out of their bodies, the blood in the sand as brilliant as the strange patterns on the feathered arrows, colorful markings from a tribe Cabeza had not yet met on his travels.

# THE GRANDFATHER HORSE

The grandfather horse was last seen galloping across the *llano* when Francisco was five years old. That morning, his father, Antonio, came running into the house. He yelled to Miranda, Francisco's mother, to come look at the grandfather horse running in their fields. She set the morning dishes on the table and followed him outside. Francisco jumped from the table and ran to join his parents. He caught sight of the ugliest yet proudest animal he had ever seen. The grandfather horse reared up on its hind legs and let out one of the most disturbing neighs Francisco had ever heard. Old scars and wounds were visible on its gray hide—the identifying mark of the grandfather horse. It turned in tight circles and kicked dirt into the air. Antonio hesitated before approaching the horse. He wanted to open the gate to the corral, hoping it would run in. The previous time the grandfather horse had appeared, many things had happened. Francisco's grandmother Lucha had died, and his brother Mario was drafted into the army. When Mario returned from his service, he was killed in a car wreck outside of town, two of his drunk friends dying with him. Now, the grandfather horse ran into the corral. Antonio shut the gate and watched the wild animal as it snorted and galloped in defiant circles, its heavy legs kicking mud and grass into the air. Francisco ran to the fence and looked in. When the grandfather horse sensed the boy, it suddenly stopped running and stood in the middle of the corral, its chest heaving, huge nostrils flaring as it tried to catch its breath. The horse looked in Francisco's direction and calmed down. His father noticed and turned to look at his son without saying a word. They watched the horse, and the animal watched them. Later, Francisco's parents were quiet at the dinner table. He asked his father what he was going to do with the horse, but his father shook his head and told him to eat his dinner. That night, Francisco woke to the neighing of the horse and went to the window, expecting to see his father at the corral, but all he saw was the horse prancing inside. When he realized his parents were asleep in the other room, Francisco dressed and went outside. The horse stopped and waited. At the fence, Francisco reached into his pocket and took out an apple he had grabbed from the kitchen. The horse ate it from his hand, its ancient eyes looking beyond the boy. Francisco tried to pet it through the fence, but it reared up. The boy pulled back and heard his father come outside. He turned to find him on the porch with his rifle cocked in his arms. Francisco ran to him, hooves pounding the earth behind him. He wanted to yell "No!" as Antonio aimed the rifle at the horse. Before his father could fire, the loud splintering of wood shattered his concentration. Francisco grabbed his father by the waist, and together they watched the grandfather horse leap over the broken corral, its mane of hair a stream of fire. The horse galloped across the dark fields, its fiery neck a torch lighting the way for something Francisco and his father lost that night. For days afterward, father and son did not speak to each other. When Miranda asked about the horse, her husband refused to answer. Over the next twenty years, Francisco's parents passed away and he went to college and became a successful agricultural businessman. One summer, while visiting the farm he had inherited, he met with the foreman who oversaw Francisco's cotton fields. The foreman took him to a shed and showed him what the workers had recently uncovered. He said most of the bones were gone, but he opened a large cardboard box that held the huge petrified skull of a horse. Francisco never would have known what the bleached thing was if the foreman hadn't told him. As they held the box in their hands, the foreman pointed to the petrified teeth and told him to look closer. Francisco bent down and saw the stem of an apple core embedded between the teeth of stone, the stem as fresh and moist as the ones on the apple trees that grew abundantly on his land.

## SPANISH

Manny was punished for speaking Spanish in school. Sister Lucia made him stand in the corner, a dunce cap on his head, his throbbing knuckles stuffed inside his pants pockets, the searing pain from Sister Lucia's ruler radiating slowly from his hands. She caught him saying "Deme el lonchi." Give me the sandwich. Manny had been sitting in the cafeteria with his cousin Joe, who had grabbed Manny's lunch when they sat down. The boys on the long table got quiet when Sister Lucia stood behind the petrified Manny. She had picked up the sound of the Spanish words, though she did not know what they meant. The nun towered over the boys. None of them dared swallow the food in their mouths. Others were caught in mid-bite and would not remove their lips from the sandwiches they held in their hands. They waited for Sister Lucia to strike. She grabbed Manny by the neck and pulled him out of the chair. He spilled his carton of milk as she dragged him away, the white liquid spreading as the frozen boys let it cross the table and surround their trays. No one moved until Sister Lucia and Manny had disappeared around the corner. Then everyone jumped to escape the milk. The sister took him to the empty classroom, where she commanded him to hold his hands straight out in front of him. She whacked him hard on the knuckles with a ruler several times, Manny refusing to cry aloud as tears streamed down his face. "English only! English only!" Sister Lucia screamed at Manny. "In school you will speak English! Do you understand?" When Manny nodded, she hit him one last time and pushed him to the corner. He stood there as she placed the yellow dunce cap on his head and pushed his nose where the two walls met. Manny could smell old chalk dust in the confined space and tried to stop crying. In a few minutes he heard his classmates return from lunch. A few giggles and smirks greeted his back. A couple of the boys whispered, "Hey, Manny. Turn around." If he did, he would suffer another beating. Manny stood there with his nose against the cold plaster of the wall. He listened as Sister Lucia started the math lesson. The fourth-graders were working on their subtraction tables, and the nun had each student stand and recite the numbers. If you gave a wrong answer after subtracting the ones she gave you, you stayed after school to write the corrections several times on the board. Manny listened as no one gave wrong answers. Then he heard the first numbers in Spanish. "Dos." "Cuatro." "Uno. "Siete." Four different voices answered the sister in Spanish. There was an enormous silence in the room until three and then four more voices answered, "Tres." "Cinco." And on and on. The chorus of Spanish numbers made Manny turn slowly around, his red eyes and blurred vision greeting the sight of Sister Lucia dropping her math cards on the floor. Half his classmates, the ones who had answered in Spanish, stood defiantly by their desks. The sister's face was redder than Manny's eyes. She sat back in the chair behind her desk. Manny removed the dunce cap from his head, dropped it on the floor, and walked quietly to his desk. He did not sit, but stood next to it. Sister Lucia covered her face with her hands and bowed her head down on her desk. She sat there for a long time until Sister Delia, the head nun of the school, walked briskly into the room. The students sat down. She comforted Sister Lucia quietly, whispered something to her, and held her by the shoulders as she led her out of the room. The class had no teacher for almost half an hour. During that time, the students sat quietly at their desks, not a single one turning to another triumphantly. Then a nun they had never seen before entered the room. She was short and fat, and some of the students wanted to laugh. "My name is Sister Patricia. I'm your new teacher. The first rule I have is no Spanish in my classroom. Does everybody understand?" Before anyone could answer, she picked up her math book and told them the page number where she wanted them to begin.

# THE LEGEND

The legend says Martita rose from the dead and gave Pentito his shadow. She came into his room one night with a fistful of flowers from her grave. She blessed his sleeping head and made sure his shadow was secure in mind and spirit. She waved the yellow petals over his closed eyes and prayed to Cristo to take care of his family. Pentito's brother was missing in Vietnam, and she had to bless Pentito's shadow so that his brother would return to his family without harm. Three months before this night, Martita was shot and killed in a drive-by shooting in the neighborhood. Pentito was the gunman, aiming at Cinto, Martita's boy. Martita knows this as she stands over the sleeping young man. She waves the driest flower over his mouth, holds it two inches from his chubby face, the tattoos on his arms glowing in the dark. The legend has it that Martita had come to Pentito's bedside every night since her murder. It says Pentito awoke one time to the blackest night he had ever seen. He stumbled for the lamp. When he turned it on, furniture in his room had been moved. He reached for his gun, went to the window, and looked out at the blackest trees and a street with no lights. Even his car in his father's driveway was painted black. Pentito rubbed his eyes and saw his shadow get in and out of the car. Out of impulse, he raised the gun but knew he was watching himself. He blinked and there was nothing there. The tale says Pentito participated

in four other drive-bys, wounding six people and killing two before being caught and sent to prison. His shadow escaped from
prison after three years. It made its way back to the neighborhood
but hesitated to enter any houses on Pentito's block because the
shadow could sense Martita's presence. It wandered the streets
at night, but no one saw it or noticed how the street lamps kept
burning out that year. Martita's flowers floated across the cool
summer night and landed in the cactus gardens of several neighbors, that season of the shadow's escape. By the time the neighbors watered their plants that rarely needed watering, Martita's
petals were dust, her fingertips tracing rows of dirt in the clay
pots. The myth is built around Martita haunting the neighborhood boys without giving them their shadows, except for Pentito, the chosen one. Some of them stayed in the gang, others got
shot, a couple survived high school to get drafted and sent to Vietnam. One of them was killed only four days into his tour. The
other made it for seven months and one week before stepping on
a booby trap and returning home with one leg and the inability
to speak. The legend points out how Pentito's brother was never
found and is officially listed as an MIA. It insists Martita eventually gave her silence to the wind and let Pentito stay incarcerated,
surviving prison until the age of thirty-four. After seventeen years
in a cell, he was stabbed in the showers. By then, the guards and
other inmates were used to the strange drawings Pentito had created on his cell walls over the years—the image of a thin, worried-
looking woman's face. The day before he was killed, Pentito drew
the largest figure of all, the woman holding a bouquet of flowers
in one of her bony hands. This entire legend is carved in micro-
scopic print on Martita's headstone. You can read the whole story
if you rub the dirt off her name and birth and death dates, then get
down on all fours and look closely where the worn stone meets

the grass on either side of the crypt. There are shadows in the dark grass, several feet of green and continuously damp grass growing in an odd island of prosperity that stands out from the rest of the dry, disintegrating rows of tombstones in the cemetery.

# POSTCARDS

In the first postcard the street where I was born is paved. When I was a boy, it was a dirt path. My grandmother's house stands in the middle of the block. The porch where I witnessed my first lightning storm dominates the photo. The second postcard, also black and white, shows a group of boys running after a pickup truck, the old vehicle throwing dust behind it as the boys reach out with their arms, trying to climb onto the back. I look closer and find I am sitting in the bed of the pickup, waving to the boys who never make it on board. The third postcard is the first colored one I find. It is a beautiful photo of the Rio Grande, the photographer focusing on the concrete bridge spanning the blue water. It is shot from a distance, so I can't make out the details of the boy and the man fishing off the bridge. I don't know who they are. The valley around the river is a bright yellow—a distorted translucent light I have never seen. The fourth postcard is one I never knew I had. I shuffle through my shoebox of postcards and hold it up. A short brown man squats in the center. There is no background color, just a naked brown man close to the ground, his face the only small thing on his huge body. Two long horns grow out of his head. They extend down his shoulders and curl like horns on a ram. In one thick hand he holds what looks like the decapitated head of a monkey. The monkey grins at the brown man. I stare at this strange picture, then quickly throw it in the pile. The fifth postcard shows another pickup truck rumbling up the street. Boys run after it. For a second I think I've pulled the same postcard, but that one sits on my desk. I realize this is different when I spot the empty bed of the pickup. In this postcard I am not sitting in the back watching the boys who can't catch me. The next postcard shows several triangles of blue light—an electric pattern like an advertisement for a computer company. On closer inspection, I see that its black background hides the image of the brown man. On this card he is dark blue, still low on his haunches. I turn the card in the light and find the monkey dancing on the back of the fat man, his head back on his body. I shake my head and flip this card away. The seventh card is a sensual image of a man and a woman, both naked. They are emerging from a bathroom shower that drips green water, different brands of shampoo bottles bordering them, green drops bouncing off their wet bodies. The man is embracing the woman, whose wet hair is stuck on the man's shoulder. They look like they have been in the shower a long time. I turn the card over and read the message scrawled in rough handwriting—"Wish you were here." It is not signed. There is no postmark. Tired of this, I pick one final postcard—a third one with the darn pickup truck. This time, the truck is parked in front of my grandmother's house, a building that is not on the earlier cards. The boys who have been chasing the vehicle are standing on the long white porch of my childhood. A couple of them point to the truck. There is no driver in the cab. I press my eyeglasses higher on my nose and squint to have a better look. Every single boy, and there are six in the picture, is me. I find the other truck cards and take a look. There I am, in the back of the pickup, in the first one. The boys are strangers. I am not in the second, and my face is nowhere in the group of running boys. I hold the last postcard and stare at my six selves. All six boys stand casually on the porch, but I can tell they are out of breath. I stare at the features I had when I was eight years old. Six images are of me dressed in shorts and sneakers. They are all me, out of breath. I have chased the pickup down my neighborhood, and now six of me stand there, waiting for the first roll of thunder, anticipating the heavy rain that is going to pound the shining body of the truck.

# CIRCLING THE TORTILLA DRAGON

Lencho circles the tortilla dragon, approaches it warily as its steam and power rise above the stove in the hot kitchen. Lencho has slain many tortilla dragons before, and this one is as powerful as those. He circles the tortilla dragon and keeps himself from making a mistake. Today he must not allow his watering mouth to touch the delicate flesh of the freshly made tortillas. He has to circle and circle because the tortilla dragon is growing larger in the kitchen. It resembles the brown and black patches Lencho has interpreted on his grandmother's tortillas since he was a boy. This dragon is a combination of those brown and black shapes that he loves to lick with his tongue, the burnt taste telling him it is a good tortilla. Lencho circles the tortilla dragon when he gets hungry, knowing the flames of this powerful force can cook him faster than they cook a tortilla. He keeps turning in the kitchen, recalls how a tortilla dragon will strike when you least expect it. Lencho pauses, and this is his first mistake. The source of his yearning lunges forward and takes him. He struggles to get away from the sharp claws and awful gas of the enormous dragon's mouth. Before he realizes what has caught him, Lencho finds himself bent over the ancient kitchen stove, his face only inches from the hot plate where his grandmother bakes her tortillas. The burner is on high as the black iron reverberates with the magnetic force that pulls Lencho within inches of his life. He tries to fight the pull toward the heat, but the dragon has him by the throat. Lencho can feel its scaly body pressing on his back, trying to flatten his face on the hot plate like a tortilla he will never eat. Suddenly, it happens. The tortilla dragon releases its grip, and Lencho is thrown across the kitchen. He tumbles backward over a chair and lands in a heap against a corner. He is dazed but looks up in time to see heavy smoke rising from the stove. A tortilla is burning. He struggles to his feet and makes it to the stove. In his rush to save the burning tortilla that wasn't there when the dragon tried to fry his face, Lencho momentarily forgets the creature in the room. As he pulls the scorched thing from the hot plate, the thick smell of burnt flour overcomes him. He turns in time to meet the massive tortilla dragon. Lencho shoves the burned tortilla into the creature's open mouth. The black chips and ashes choke the dragon. It rears back and knocks the kitchen table aside, and the room fills with smoke. He can hardly see, but Lencho thinks the dragon has crawled out the front door. He grabs two fresh tortillas off the stack his grandmother made a half hour earlier and runs outside. It is too late. The dragon has disappeared. Lencho eats the two tortillas as the burnt air behind him reshapes itself, the first long curves of heavy wings starting to appear in the blue smoke of the quiet kitchen.

# THE JALAPEÑO CONTEST

Freddy and his brother Tesoro have not seen each other in five years, and they sit at the kitchen table in Freddy's house and have a jalapeño contest. A large bowl of big green and orange jalapeño peppers sits between the two brothers. A salt shaker and two small glasses of beer accompany this feast. When Tesoro nods his head, the two men begin to eat the raw jalapeños. The contest is to see which man can eat more peppers. It is a ritual from their father, but the two brothers tried it only once, years ago. Both quit after two peppers and laughed it off. This time, things are different. They are older and have to prove a point. Freddy eats his first one more slowly than Tesoro, who takes two bites to finish his and is now on his second. Neither says anything, though a close study of each man's face would tell you that the sudden burst of jalapeño energy does not waste time in changing the eater's perception of reality. Freddy works on his second as Tesoro rips into his fourth. Freddy is already sweating from his head and is surprised to see that Tesoro's fat face has not changed its steady, consuming look. Tesoro's long black hair is neatly combed, and not one bead of sweat has popped out. He is the first to sip from the beer before hitting his fifth jalapeño. Freddy leans back as the table begins to sway in his damp vision. He coughs, and a sharp pain rips through his chest. Tesoro attempts to laugh at his brother, but Freddy sees it is something else. As Freddy finishes his third jalapeño, Tesoro begins to breathe faster upon swallowing his sixth. The contest momentarily stops as both brothers shift in their seats and the sweat pours down their faces. Freddy clutches his stomach as he reaches for a fourth delight. Tesoro has not taken his seventh, and it is clear to Freddy that his brother is suffering big-time. There is a bright blue bird sitting on Tesoro's head, and Tesoro is struggling to laugh because Freddy has a huge red spider crawling on top of his head. Freddy wipes the sweat from his eyes and finishes his fourth pepper. Tesoro sips more beer, sprinkles salt on the tip of his jalapeño, and bites it down to the stem. Freddy, who has not touched his beer, stares in amazement as two Tesoros sit in front of him. They both rise hastily, their beer guts pushing the table against Freddy, who leans back as the two Tesoros waver in the kitchen light. Freddy hears a tremendous fart erupt from his brother, who sits down again. Freddy holds his fifth jalapeño and can't breathe. Tesoro's face is purple, but the blue bird has been replaced by a burning flame of light that weaves over Tesoro's shiny head. Freddy is convinced that he is having a heart attack as he watches his brother fight for breath. Freddy bites into his fifth as Tesoro flips his eighth jalapeño into his mouth, stem and all. This is it. Freddy goes into convulsions and drops to the floor as he tries to reach for his glass of beer. He shakes on the dirty floor as the huge animal that is Tesoro pitches forward and throws up millions of jalapeño seeds all over the table. The last thing Freddy sees before he passes out is his brother's body levitating above the table as an angel, dressed in green jalapeño robes, floats into the room, extends a hand to Tesoro, and floats away with him. When Freddy wakes minutes later, he gets up and makes it to the bathroom before his body lets go through his pants. As he reaches the bathroom door, he turns and gazes upon the jalapeño plants growing healthy and large on the kitchen table, thick peppers hanging under their leaves, their branches immersed in the largest pile of yellow jalapeño seeds Freddy has ever seen.

# THE PROPERTIES OF MAGIC

Augustino learned the properties of magic when he found a broken rosary on the playground and turned it in to Sister Delina. The sister stared at him without saying a word and took the broken rosary from his outstretched hand. He left her classroom worried that she thought he had broken it. Augustino studied the properties of magic when he went to church alone, knelt before La Virgen de Guadalupe, and lit one candle in the rows of dozens of unlit candles. He prayed, then opened his eyes to find two whole rows of burning candles. He made the sign of the cross and quickly left the church. Augustino was taught the properties of magic when he awoke in the middle of the night to find a headless man standing at the foot of his bed. The man, dressed in an old army uniform, reached into his empty neck and pulled out a piñata of a donkey like the one Augustino had been given by his parents on his fifth birthday. Gasping for air, Augustino lay back on the bed and wanted to scream. He stayed calm, then peered out from the blankets. There was no one there. Augustino contemplated the properties of magic the day the sparrow flew into his room and touched all four corners with a rapid fluttering of wings. When Augustino looked up from doing his homework at his desk, the sparrow was hovering over a drawing of a river and mountain he had colored in school that day. Augustino stood and waved his arms, and the sparrow found its way out the window. Augustino realized the properties of magic when he went to shut the window and found two ants carrying a dead honeybee across the sill. He bent down and watched the struggling insects move the heavy bee, inch by inch. He let them cross, until a breeze from the open window blew the ants and their meal over the ledge and outside. Augustino believed in the properties of magic when his parents screamed at each other and his father left one night, never to return. For the first two weeks that his father was gone, Augustino waited on the porch, rocking quietly on the old white swing. His father never returned. Late one night, near the end of the two weeks of waiting, Augustino watched from the swing as a blue light hovered in the alley across the street. At first he thought it was the headlights from a car, perhaps his father's, moving between the houses. As he stopped swinging and stared, the blue light traced patterns on the adobe walls, lifted high above the dark houses, and came straight at Augustino. Before he could react, the blue light exploded in front of his eyes like a Fourth of July sparkler, then disappeared. Augustino used the properties of magic when he rose from the swing, bent down, and picked up the broken rosary on the ground. He cupped it in his hands, pressing harder to feel the warmth, and thought he heard his father's voice down the street. When his mother called him to come inside, Augustino placed the mended rosary in his pocket and opened the screen door for the last time that night.

# THE CHINESE RESTAURANT

I meet my father for lunch in the Chinese restaurant after not having seen him for eight years. He gets out of the car in the parking lot, and I am stunned at how thin and wrinkled he looks. We hug awkwardly and enter the place. I notice he has a slight limp in his walk that he never had before. An accident or old age? We sit in the empty place and open our menus. I look at the other tables with their neat red tablecloths and the perfectly set napkins at each. My father, divorced from my mother now for almost twenty years, asks me how the family is doing as we try to decide what we will order. I fill him in on the lives of my mother and sister as the waitress approaches. She is a young Chinese woman, and she sets glasses of water on our table. Without asking if I am ready to order, my father orders for us—two of the lunch specials with steamed rice. I feel strange having a meal with my father. We have had little contact since the divorce. Suddenly, the kitchen doors fly open and an old Chinese man who looks like the cook runs out. Right behind him, an old Chinese woman emerges with a large cleaver in her hand. She chases the cook around the tables, both of them screaming in Chinese. My father says he knows both of them, that he has eaten here many times. I am in town visiting, so I knew nothing about this. The old man grips a table and pushes it in the path of the old woman, who my father says is the cook's wife. She whacks the table with the cleaver. Pieces of red tablecloth and wood fly into the air. The old man comes up our aisle, and I want to get out of the way. He pauses to shake my father's hand. His wife is stumbling over chairs and can't reach him. The cook waves goodbye and disappears into the kitchen. The old woman, out of breath, heads slowly after him, her weapon down at her side. I look at my father, who is not disturbed by this. I don't feel like eating anymore, but my father begins to tell me about the heart attack he suffered four years ago—an event no one in the family knew about. I sit in stone silence and listen to him describe the ordeal. In his typical fashion, he has kept his life over the last two decades a secret from us, his first family. I almost jump out of my chair as the kitchen doors slam open and our young waitress jogs out, balancing our plates in her hands. The screams of the old woman echo through the swinging doors. Our waitress does not spill a single grain of rice or an almond from our chicken. She sets them on our table and runs out of the restaurant. My father begins to eat peacefully, but I don't have a chance to look at my steaming plate because the old man staggers out of the kitchen and falls dead on the floor, the meat cleaver embedded in his back. My father looks over, blinks once, and continues eating. I try to stand, but my father's cold hand pushes me back down. He nods at my plate and keeps eating. I stare at him, then turn and watch as the old woman appears triumphantly, steps over her husband's body, and comes toward us. I lean back in my chair in horror. The only thing in her hand is the water pitcher. She smiles at my father with the look a regular customer deserves and refills our glasses. My father thanks her as she turns, goes to the body, yanks the cleaver out, and goes into the kitchen. My father looks at me. His expression tells me he is annoyed that I have not touched my food. We have not exchanged one word since the old man went down. Again, my father nods at my plate. With a shaking hand, I pick up my fork and stick it into the mound of rice and almond chicken. I want to hear the distant sound of police sirens, but all I hear are the sounds of pots and pans in the kitchen. My father begins to tell me about his second wife as I eat my food in silence.

## SPACESHIP

Santo climbs over the rocks of the arroyo, comes up on level ground, and there it is. A UFO hovers low off the desert floor fifty yards away. Santo catches his breath and takes a drink from his canteen as he watches the silent object. It is the size of a pickup, oval-shaped, with blue lights blinking underneath. The body is a turquoise-colored metal. Santo can't see windows on the thing. The boy and the spaceship face each other for a long time. He feels the minutes go by as the sweat runs down his neck into his T-shirt, even down his legs. It must be one hundred degrees in the desert. Santo looks at his watch. Three o'clock—the hottest part of a June afternoon. He takes another drink of water. Then the thing begins to move slowly toward him. Santo wants to run, but he will fall down the arroyo if he moves. He looks to his left, then right. Cactus and piles of rocks block both directions. The spaceship rises higher as it comes near the boy. There is deafening silence. Santo's legs are frozen to the hot ground, and he can feel the heat through his sneakers. Even though he is wearing sunglasses, Santo shades his eyes with his hands as he looks up. When the object is directly above him, the blue lights stop blinking. A square door opens in its belly, and something drops out. Santo skips aside as a rectangular box slowly comes down and onto the ground with a mechanical hiss. The box is the same turquoise hue as the mother ship. It sits in the sand. Santo can't get himself to run away. The lid of the box opens. Santo approaches carefully, keeping one eye on the quiet thing in the sky. He stands over the box and finds a leather scrapbook inside. Without knowing why, he lifts the heavy book out. The metal box shoots straight up and is swallowed by the mother ship. Santo doesn't blink an eye at this because he is flipping through the scrapbook filled with yellow newspaper clippings. They contain headlines and articles about the 1947 crash of a spacecraft in Roswell, New Mexico, fifty miles east of where Santo is standing. He turns page after page and smells the ancient glue and crumbling newspaper. As he strains to see what the hovering spaceship is doing, a spark of light snaps across the sky. Santo falls, clutching the scrapbook, his legs giving way as he tumbles down the arroyo. He rolls and rolls, dirt in his mouth, thorns cutting his legs. He comes to a stop at the bottom and lies there a long time. The scrapbook has landed open in the dirt. When he is able to sit up and catch his breath, he leans over to look at the photograph open to the sky. It shows a father and son standing on a dirt street. They are holding scraps of metal with strange symbols on them. The caption says something about the Roswell crash. Santo gazes at the man and boy. He does not know who they are. When he rereads the caption, it identifies the location of the photo as the town where Santo was born. He climbs out of the arroyo, leaving the scrapbook at the bottom with some of his gear. When he reaches the top, there is no spaceship, only a dark object on the ground. Santo goes to it. It is a second scrapbook. He picks it up, but this one smells different. He opens the brand new leather to find blank page after blank page, the thick book so light in his hands.

## IN THE RUINS

I try to climb out of the adobe ruins, but these rooms, walls, and caved-in roofs keep me inside. I move through dust and broken boards, place my dirty hands on the cold walls. Turquoise-and-white plaster covers sections of the mud walls. I climb out of the shattered doorway and meet tumbleweeds and fallen roof beams. Mounds of disintegrated adobe hold me down, window frames and glass missing from the cuts in the walls, the openings blocked by layers of brick. I want to move from exploded room to exploded corridor, but the light filtering through the sunken roof holds me back. Falling to my knees, I find the graffiti and handprints on the walls, their white paint hard to spot, their location near the floor making me think they were drawn by a child. The men and women dance together, their stick arms pointing to the sky. A fence has been drawn around them. The handprints are small, but they reach for an opening, a way out of the adobe. I stand up and bring dust and a loose brick down. It crashes near my foot and creates a cloud of brown and white as I cough and roll into the corridor. Glass from broken beer bottles crinkles beneath my boots. I step on a loose board that breaks, send my foot through the floor, my ankle caught momentarily when I move toward the lowest ray of light I see. Again, tumbleweeds, boards with nails, and huge slabs of adobe block my way. I push some of them aside, but this action brings part of the roof down. More debris falls in my path, so I give up going in that direction. In the growing darkness, I find a standing door, the only one I have seen in this destruction. It is painted a deep green and has an old ivory door handle. I try to turn it, but it won't move. I bend down and see light beneath the door. Feeling like I am running out of breath, I grab the nearest heavy board, take a few steps back, then lunge forward. The old wood of the door splinters as the beam goes through. More roof falls on the other side, but here is a way out. I stick my arm through the jagged splinters and unlock the door. I step into a large room where piles of adobe, broken chairs, an old bathtub, two car tires, and dozens of broken beer bottles greet me. The light filters through the boarded window on the far side of the room. The floor is pure dirt, the only room I have found without a wooden floor. I move toward the blocked window and stumble over torn paper bags, their sand spilling out, one of them containing a torn package of condoms. Has someone been here recently? How did they get out? I kick the bag away and keep my balance by holding onto a tiny kitchen table near the window. As I grab the first board on the window frame, I notice something on the table, reach down and pick up a matchbook. I flip the blank cover open, find a few matches, and put them in my pocket. I tear two boards off, but they expose an iron grill. The air in the room grows thicker. I reach for the matches, light one, and toss it in a pile of tumbleweeds in the corner. They ignite in a second, their dryness and the pure stillness of the adobe popping around me. I want the fire to spread upward and burn the roof, but I have to move back into the corridor as the flames follow me instead. I hear sirens in the distance, but there is no one out there. These rooms are in the middle of a row of ruined houses, the cotton and lettuce fields around them long abandoned, the encroaching smoke signaling this is not the way out of their crumbling. I reach and grab a roof beam near a shattered streak of light. As I pull myself up and breathe fresh air through the opening, my legs feel the heat. I press my mouth to the narrow cut and hang there. My eyes adjust to the light above me as I spot two white handprints on the wood near my face. I recognize the fine detail on the palms someone caught precisely in white and release my grip.

# HOW THE BRUJO STOLE THE MOON

When the moon came close to the earth one year, the *brujo* told his people to stare at the bright white ball. He wanted the entire village to come out of their houses and, upon his signal, to look at the moon. The ceremony would not take long because the brujo wanted the moon for himself, its light to wash its burning force into his heart. He needed to possess the moon to be able to heal and know what the future held. By taking the moon, he could prevent families from leaving every time something bad happened in the village. Running into the desert, they wandered for days, most never returning. As the moon drew closer each night, the brujo was ready to take it and become the strongest man in the village. He built a huge fire in the middle of the plaza and shouted strange things in the darkness. One by one, the people came out of their houses and walked toward the tall flames. The brujo was draped in a long robe the color of the river — bright blue and orange swirls ran down his bony shoulders. He wore a tall headdress of peacock and owl feathers. He depended on the peacock feathers for their magnetic force. As a brujo, he was allowed to take one owl in his lifetime and use its feathers. He had woven the smaller owl feathers among the reflecting blue circles of the peacock feathers. He owned many headdresses, but this one was special and rarely appeared in his many rituals. He waited until every villager had crowded into a tight circle around the fire. Raising both arms, he tilted his head back until he could see the burning moon. His arms started to shake, and the people grew quiet as they stared at their brujo. His body kept shaking as he fought to stay on his feet. The rising flames brought his feathers to life. They waved in many colors, the delicate shapes taken from birds washing the brujo with light, protecting him from the intense heat. His head was thrown back, his face contorted. The people stood transfixed as a tube of flame separated itself from the fire. The brujo opened his eyes when the tower of fire rose into the night. It was the comet he had been waiting for. He knew the fire that flew toward the moon was the right sign. The instant the comet disappeared into the sky, the entire village fell into a trance. The brujo waited as every man, woman, and child lay down on the ground and slept. He stepped over several people on his way to his shack. Before going inside, he looked at the moon. It was a round yellow ball hurtling toward earth. No one in the village was allowed to go inside his shack. They would have been surprised to find nothing but a wooden table and a small cot. There were no signs of the medicine and rituals he performed. A couple of cloth bags that contained his robes lay in a corner. Otherwise, the room was empty. The brujo reached into the sack and pulled out a tiny, wooden doll that had been carved with no arms. He closed his eyes and held the doll to his chest. His heart beat faster. When he opened his eyes, the walls of the room glowed brightly. He threw open the door to a blinding light. The burning force of the approaching moon turned his hair and face white. As he held his arms over his head, he lost his eyesight and dropped the doll in the dirt. Moonlight blistered the ground as the doll disappeared. Rows of green plants and fresh vegetables appeared instantly around the village. People awoke to find themselves in rich fields of corn, onions, and grapes. They looked up as the distant moon changed shape. Some claimed they saw the face of the brujo on the moon. A few ran into their homes to hide from the night skies. They searched the village for the brujo but could not find him. He had disappeared into the universe. The people decided the moon was the back of his head, that he was facing away because he had forgotten them. They claimed a face appeared for a few seconds, then turned away again as the moon moved from white to a deep yellow. It kept this color until the first rays of sunlight told the people the new day was going to begin without their brujo. As the men of the village stood among the riches in their fields, they decided to harvest what had been given to them. They worked for hours in the hot sun. When they went to sleep, they turned to the sky and thought of the brujo. They were convinced he was up there. When they looked up before falling asleep each night, the moon came down to earth and rolled across the fields in a dance only the brujo knew.

*Part Two*

# EDUARDO

Ten-year-old Eduardo Moises stood on the bank of the dry Rio Grande and watched his mongrel dog, Loco, splash across the muddy puddles of water on the river bottom. He called to Loco when it ran up the opposite bank and disappeared in the tall reeds. Eduardo pulled his baseball cap more tightly onto his head and ran across the river, his sneakers sinking into the mud with a loud plop-plop, his fast legs leaving a trail of flying water behind him. Eduardo grabbed a stick and followed Loco through the yellow grass. He spotted the dog as it crawled under the rusting frame of an old car that sat in the middle of an unplanted cotton field. Eduardo stopped several yards from the car as the mild fear and excitement of adventure ran through him. He had not forgotten about the skeleton of the cow he had found at the bottom of an abandoned well two weeks ago. He'd almost fallen through the thin wood covering while chasing Loco away from the buzzing flies. One of Eduardo's legs had broken through the wood. He'd pushed himself up and peered through the hole to discover the large bones ten feet below. He'd run home and had hardly been able to explain what he'd seen to his mother.

This time, he hesitated before approaching the junked car. He looked over his shoulder toward the river, but there was nothing to look at. There had been days since he'd stumbled upon the skeleton when Eduardo thought someone was watching him. The figure would vanish before he could turn around. There was never anyone there. In the distance, the Sandia Mountains were red in the early morning light. Eduardo wondered if anyone had seen him leave the neighborhood so early in the day. He stepped up to the passenger side of the metal frame and looked through the shattered window. Grass grew through holes in the floorboards. He pulled on the door, but it wouldn't open.

Loco startled him when he barked and leaped out of the back of the car, pieces of seat stuffing clinging to his dirty white fur. The dog had spotted a jackrabbit and had chased it across the field, disappearing into an abandoned house at the other end of the field. The adobe structure had one wall completely down and the door hanging by one hinge. Eduardo and Loco had passed this way before, but this was the first time the dog had gone into the ruins. Eduardo gazed at the four huge cottonwood trees that rose in the yard. Their enormous gray trunks defied the thick wall of tumbleweeds clustering around them as they surrounded the shattered house. As he neared the place, he noticed the rope and wooden swing that hung from the farthest tree. The small piece of wood that served as the seat leaned crookedly in the air, too high for a small boy to climb on.

He spotted a strange sight on the tree closest to him and moved into the shadows of the branches to get a better look. The high wall of tumbleweeds prevented him from standing directly under the tree. He squinted into the early sun and studied the wooden birdcage that hung from one of the branches. It swayed in the breeze with the tiny door open, and he wondered what kind of bird would be attracted to such an ugly cage. His thoughts were broken by Loco's barks from inside the house. Eduardo climbed over old car tires, rusted tin cans, and enormous ant hills to reach the broken porch. He looked behind him again because Loco's bark had brought back the feeling of being watched.

Again, there was no one behind him. He stepped carefully on

the rotting boards and paused in the open doorway of the dark, damp room. It was empty except for a wooden shelf standing against the far wall. Dust hung in the air and reflected off sharp beams of sunlight breaking through holes in the ceiling. Some of the floorboards had fallen through. Thick grass grew through the cracks, and tumbleweeds piled themselves in the corners. The lone window was a diamond-shaped cut in the wall, the glass broken long ago. The cut held an intricately designed wooden frame.

Eduardo went to the shelf and found an object of a kind he had never seen, a small barrel about eight inches deep, carved out of heavy wood with colored symbols painted on its sides. He lifted it off the shelf and looked inside. It was empty except for a few spider webs and dirt at the bottom. He turned it gently in his hands as Loco ran out the door. Eduardo lost interest in chasing the dog as he studied the symbols. They were painted red, blue, and green.

He clutched the object to his chest for a few seconds, then placed it gently on the shelf. He wanted to keep the thing but felt chills on his arms and face. Taking it would be wrong. Eduardo had never stolen anything from anyone. The various pieces of junk he brought home—old car parts, pieces of glass and wood, and odd-shaped bottles—were all picked up from abandoned places. If he took this wonderful thing home, his mother would ask where he'd gotten it. With her superstitions against the unknown, Eduardo knew she would not let him keep it. Those strange markings on the barrel could not sit in her house alongside religious calendars, votive candles, and statues of many saints. As Eduardo thought about his mother and her crucifixes and rosaries, the feeling of doing something wrong went away.

Eduardo turned to leave, then paused to look at the object one more time. He stepped out onto the porch and wondered what time it was. Loco barked in the distance. Eduardo was distracted by movement in the trees. He looked up at the swing. It was moving along an arc that sent a thin shadow sweeping across the yard. Who had pushed the swing? He looked at the birdcage on its shorter rope and saw that the door was now closed. Loco's next bark sounded closer. Eduardo ran back into the house, tripped on one of the dirt mounds in the floor, then got up and grabbed the bright barrel from the shelf. He ran outside and looked around, but all he saw was the emptiness of the cotton field beyond the trees.

Then he saw the old man sitting in the shade under one of the cottonwoods. Several tumbleweeds had been tossed aside to make room to sit against the trunk. The man gave Eduardo a toothless smile. The boy tensed, ready to run for the river with his treasure, but the stranger waved a hand in a peaceful gesture. Loco appeared out of the weeds and growled at the sitting figure. The dog kept growling, hesitant to move closer. Eduardo stood behind the dog. The old man was not the figure, Eduardo was sure, who had been following him for several days. The man waved Eduardo forward, but Eduardo shook his head at the invitation and drew closer to Loco.

The old man wore a pair of tiny sunglasses like the kind Eduardo had seen blind people wear. Eduardo gripped the barrel tighter in his arms. The old man reached into his ragged shirt and pulled out a small flute. Eduardo relaxed a bit, fascinated at the sight of this man with long white hair and dirty clothes playing a flute. He noticed that the man's gnarled toes stuck out through torn moccasins. The notes of the flute sent Loco into a frenzy. The dog barked rapidly, kicked dirt behind it, and seemed to want to jump on the old man.

"Shut up!" Eduardo shouted. Loco whimpered and sniffed the ground.

The man stopped playing for an instant, then begin again. He blew a low, rolling note that drifted across the stillness in the trees. His face was wrinkled and very red. Eduardo wondered whether the barrel belonged to him. He stopped playing and motioned for Eduardo to step closer. Eduardo shook his head. His mother had warned him about talking to strangers, but this mysterious person was different. His looks reminded Eduardo of the Navajos who lived at the far end of the town in a separate neighborhood from his family and friends. There were four Navajo families, but he did not recall seeing this man among them.

"Who are you?" Eduardo asked in a low voice. Loco whimpered at his feet and stood his ground.

The old man grinned. Eduardo moved close enough to study the worn face of brown skin. The stranger removed his sunglasses and rubbed his eyes. "My name is Emilio Two Moons."

Eduardo giggled. "Two Moons? Nobody is named Two Moons." He wanted to run.

"That is my name."

"I don't believe it." Eduardo stepped back a few feet.

"Don't go," the old man said, then coughed twice. "Come closer."

"What do you want?" Eduardo asked without moving. "Do you live here?"

The old man tucked the flute into his red shirt. "No one lives here. Everybody has flown away."

"What do you mean?" Eduardo glanced at the menacing cottonwoods above them.

"Look." The old man pointed to the swing and the birdcage. "They have all flown away. This house is empty, and I see you have a gift from the house."

For the first time Eduardo panicked at having taken the barrel. "I found it," he explained quickly and bowed his head.

"I know," the stranger said. He began to stand.

Loco growled and started to go at him, but Eduardo pushed the dog back with his foot. "Go, Loco!"

At the command the dog bounded off toward the river. The old man smiled at the animal's quick obedience. Eduardo backed up as the man stood on shaky legs, supporting himself with one bony arm against the tree. His baggy brown pants were caked with mud and torn at both knees.

"It is a nice gift," the man continued. "Would you like to have it?"

"Does it belong to you?"

The old man shook his head. "No." He let go of the tree. "If you want to keep it, you must do me a favor."

"What?"

"Tell me what it says."

Eduardo looked down at the symbols on the barrel. "I don't know."

"Then why did you take it?" The old man put his sunglasses back on.

Eduardo didn't know what to say. He wanted to run as fast as Loco toward the river and not let go of his find. Why did this stranger want to take it from him? The man started to approach Eduardo but, after a few steps, fell to his knees. He knelt there, holding his stomach with both hands, his white hair bright in the air, his face turning red with pain.

Eduardo went to him and knelt down, frightened. "Are you okay?"

"Don't worry," the old man hissed through his teeth. "I am too old for this."

"For what?"

Emilio Two Moons allowed Eduardo to help him sit back against the tree. The boy felt the man's thin, bony back and smelled tobacco on his tattered clothes.

"I'm too old to be out here trying to collect things like you do. I should go live with my son, who keeps begging me."

"Where do you live?" Eduardo asked. He stood and clutched the barrel tighter.

"I've been looking for a place like this," Emilio gestured at the ruins. "I used to live in a house like this near Laguna Pueblo, but it burned down many years ago."

"Are you hurt?" Eduardo asked and sat on the ground out of the man's reach.

"Yes," the stranger smiled. "It is an old hurt. It will go away in a few minutes. People have left too many things behind, but it is good to see that boys like you will always find them and keep us alive."

Eduardo didn't understand what he was saying and wondered if the man was trying to tell him it was wrong to take the barrel. "Do you need a doctor?"

"No, it would not do any good." He sounded like he was breathing easier.

"I need to go," Eduardo told him when he heard Loco bark, far away.

"Why are you taking that with you if you have not told yourself that you know what it means?"

The conversation confused Eduardo further. "I asked if it was yours."

"No, it is not mine, but it belongs in that house if no one knows what it is for. Perhaps the earth needs to take it because the earth made it."

Eduardo decided the old man was crazy, but the words made him decide to return the barrel.

"Has someone taken it before?" Eduardo asked.

"Yes, some bring it back. Some never return it."

Eduardo was totally confused. He had the thing right here. "Are you always here to guard this?"

"No, this is the first time I have come this far up the river. The birdcage and the swing are waiting for birds and boys like you to come live here again. There are too many empty houses these days. The gift is the last thing left. This house will forgive you."

Eduardo nodded. He wanted their conversation to end. He thought the old man was lying and did live here. It was the only way he could understand that it was important to return the object. The stranger scared him, and he had no choice. As Loco barked again in the distance, Eduardo returned to the ruins. He stepped over the broken boards and heard a rustling among the tumbleweeds in the room. He stopped in front of the shelf as a huge green lizard with a bright red head appeared from under the tumbleweeds. He had never seen such an enormous lizard. It must have been two feet long. It was not the same kind as the tiny green and gray lizards that ran everywhere in the desert. The huge thing raised its head a few inches, trembled like lizards do, then darted under the rubble.

Eduardo placed the barrel on the shelf and quickly stepped outside. The old man was gone. Eduardo ran around the trees and through the tumbleweeds, but there was no sign of him. He looked up at the birdcage. The door was open, and the swing on the rope was petrified in stillness. Eduardo ran onto the high bank of the river for a better view of the house and trees. From up there he could see the cottonwoods and the roof of the crumbling place. There was no one in sight, the field next to the house flat and empty. He wondered if the stranger had gone inside to take the barrel for himself.

Loco's barking made him turn as the dog ran along the bank.

It chased something into the tall cattails. Eduardo jumped into the shallow, muddy river, the mud sticking to his shoes as he hopped across. He stopped on the other side and tried to get another view of the house, but now he was too far away. He ran home with Loco, crossing two fields before coming to the first streets of the town. He walked past his school, the yard empty in the middle of July. As he came up his street, he saw Tony and Pelon playing basketball next door to his house. Loco ran up to his friends, but before Eduardo could join them and tell them what he'd seen, they heard sirens in the distance.

"Hey, where have you been?" Tony yelled. He threw the basketball. "We've been looking for you. Your mother said you took off."

Eduardo caught the ball with a grunt and took a shot that missed. "Yeah," he said. Loco chased the basketball excitedly, then ran home when Eduardo's mother came out onto the porch.

"Eduardo!" she yelled. "Where have you been? I've been worried. What are those sirens?" The wailing grew closer.

The boys saw the two fire trucks speed past the school, a rare sight since the small town never had fires.

"Lets go look!" Tony shouted, starting to head for his bike.

"No! Stay here!" Eduardo's mother commanded the boys. "Don't you know it is bad luck to follow fire trucks to a fire?"

They stood under Tony's basketball hoop and watched the vehicles disappear in clouds of dust. When Eduardo saw the bright green trucks turn down Alba Street, he realized where they were going. He ran to his garage and grabbed his bike.

"Eduardo! I told you to stay here!" his mother cried. "Come back here!"

Tony and Pelon stood in shock as Eduardo disobeyed his mother and rapidly pedaled away.

His mother's cries disappeared behind him, their sound covered by the sirens and the wind shrieking in Eduardo's ears as he raced down the empty streets. He crossed the Alba bridge over the river. Thick black smoke rose through the cottonwoods. The pavement ended on the other side of the bridge, and Eduardo's tires kicked up rocks and dirt. Three sheriff's cars blocked the entrance to the field and the burning house. He screeched to a halt and almost fell off the skidding bike.

Eduardo panted hard, trying to catch his breath as he watched the ruins go up in flames. He looked around in panic for the old man. Eduardo felt the heat of the fire on his head. The smoke rose hundreds of feet into the air, drawing villagers to the scene in cars and on foot. The deputies kept them back. Eduardo climbed on his bike and pedaled slowly along the police barrier. He searched for the old man in the small crowd, but he was not there. Eduardo swung his bike toward the inferno and raced across the field.

"Hey, come back here!" a deputy shouted, and ran after him.

Eduardo crossed the hard earth of the field and approached the burning trees, the heat making him cough and jump off the bike. Smoke stung his eyes. Several firemen with huge hoses noticed him and pointed. The last thing he saw before the deputy grabbed him was the birdcage hanging from the tree in flames. The man picked up Eduardo by the waist, grabbed the handlebars of the bike, and pulled him to safety. Eduardo heard loud pops, shouts from the firemen, and a bubbling sound that seemed to come from the house. As they crossed the field, Eduardo raised his head in time to see the roof of the house explode in sparks. It fell with a crash as the deputy set him on the ground.

"Don't ever do that again!" he scolded Eduardo. "Go on home! It's over!"

He let Eduardo have his bike and stood over him. Eduardo rode slowly away, the heat pushing against his back. As he reached Alba Street, he thought he heard the sound of a flute. He stopped the bike, dismounted, and waited for the old man to walk out of the smoke. He thought he heard the flute again, but he concluded it was the wind above the burning trees. Then the sound of another siren smothered everything. Eduardo watched another fire truck lumber to a stop, its lights flashing, as the smoke billowed above the men crossing the field.

# MOUNTAIN

Johnny de la Rosa jumped out of the jeep and held onto the bumper as he looked over the edge of the narrow road. Gazing down the steep mountain, he felt a twitch in his knees. They must have climbed several miles up the dirt trail before it became too narrow. The rear wheels were half a foot from the edge. Johnny could see the Rio Grande below, a muddy ribbon that wound around the west side of Cristo Rey, the mountain he was driving up with his brother Tony and their friend Juan Escandon. From that height, El Paso was a flat haze in the distance. Below them, the scattered houses of Sunland Park and Anapra, New Mexico, disappeared to the north.

"I thought you fixed this part!" Tony yelled to Juan. Tony was driving the jeep. Juan gave him a wide-eyed look and shook his head. In the shrieking wind, they had to yell to hear each other. They climbed carefully out of the jeep and went to the front. A large gash in the road made it impossible to drive the remaining two miles to the top of Cristo Rey.

"¡Cabrón!" Tony yelled to Juan.

"Hey, man! I was busy getting all the parts for the generator!" Juan shouted back. "*Ese* Johnny was supposed to fill the holes in the road."

Johnny came around to their side, and all three leaned against the jeep. Tony took a canteen of water and passed it around. The wind drew gusts of sand and stung their eyes. Johnny took the canteen and looked up at the huge granite statue of Christ on the cross that rose at the top of the mountain.

Tomorrow was Good Friday. The three of them were part of a Sunland Park volunteer group whose job was to make the road usable for the hundreds of people who would make this year's annual pilgrimage. It meant filling potholes and removing rocks from the winding road. On Friday they would need to have the jeep on standby in case anyone needed to be driven off the mountain in a hurry. This year the group had raised money to buy a generator to keep the forty-two-foot statue lighted on Good Friday night. Cristo Rey mountain rose at exactly the point where Mexico, Texas, and New Mexico met. The lighted statue would be seen for miles in each of them.

A week ago, the three of them had driven the small generator to the top and had tested the floodlights. Everything had worked. They locked the generator in a metal shed near the base of the statue, planning to come back on Good Friday to set it up. They should have known better. Someone had broken into the shed and stolen the generator. The poor community, which had worked hard to raise the money for the equipment, was devastated. A last-minute fund drive in El Paso had come up with money for a replacement. Tonight, Johnny, his brother, and Juan would stay on the mountain to guard the equipment, then set it up early in the morning before the first people arrived.

Johnny looked at the cut in the road. "It rained real hard the other night. We did fix this part, but it looks like it got washed away."

"Yeah," said Tony as the wind died for a moment. "Man, it's tough this year. You know the Padre will be upset with us if we don't get it all done on time. Plus, we need this thing at the top." He banged his fist on the old 1976 jeep and pulled two shovels out of the back.

"Why don't we send Johnny up there to see if there's anything else we need to do?" Juan said. He pointed toward the cross.

More wind and dirt spun up the mountain. The outstretched arms of the crucified Christ vanished for an instant in a brown mass of swirling sand, then broke through in a span of sunlight. Johnny closed his eyes. The sight of the disappearing and reappearing cross made him dizzy in the wind.

"I thought we checked everything," Tony answered, taking one of the shovels.

"Yeah," said Juan, "but you know all the things that have happened this year. It will take awhile to fill this part. He can hike up and make sure no one has sprayed more shit on the statue."

They had spent a day last week painting over the graffiti on the base of the statue. In their many trips to the top, they had never actually seen anyone defacing the monument. Yet, most mornings when they arrived, they found fresh graffiti sprayed in a variety of bright colors.

"I'll go," Johnny said.

Tony nodded. "Take some white paint."

Johnny was glad to go up by himself, to get away from his brother, who was always telling him what to do. He grabbed a canteen, a brush, and a can of whitewash, then glanced at Juan and Tony as they started filling the gash in the road with dirt from the mountainside.

He rounded the first curve and looked back. He was out of their sight. The wind seemed stronger here on the south side of the mountain, which faced the Chihuahua desert far below. Johnny was always amazed at the view. The mountains south of Ciudad Juárez had turned a blinding brown in the early afternoon sun. He wondered what was beyond those mountains. This unexpected chance to walk up alone got him excited and gave him a sense of freedom. He had been to the statue many times to kneel and pray under it but felt self-conscious doing it in front of his brother.

Tony and Juan were constantly upset over the graffiti on the statue, but Johnny did not mind painting over it. He did it as a service to the Lord. He knew many *vatos* from Juárez crossed over the mountain and hid on it, but he also knew that kids from his own town were responsible for much of the vandalism.

He came around another sharp bend and spotted two empty beer cans in the road. He picked them up, crushed them, and stuck them in his backpack. He looked up at the cross and blinked as more dust and wind howled around him. He hoped it would not be like this on Good Friday. It was another half hour to the top if he stayed on the road. He considered climbing straight up the rough terrain, crossing over the rocks and cliffs as many people did, but this area was thick with Spanish daggers and other huge cactus. He noticed more holes in the road they would have to fill before finishing the job. He wondered if they could get the jeep to the top by nightfall.

He walked on. The wind slammed into the mountain. A huge cloud of dust twisted up the cliffs and shrieked around him. He stepped back from the edge of the trail and sat, covering his face with his jacket to wait for the storm to pass. He had never encountered such strong winds this high on the mountain. These storms normally stayed on the desert floor. He thought about Tony and Juan and wondered if they could get anything done in this wind.

Then Johnny heard a cry. At first he thought it was the wind, but the sound was human. For an instant he figured it was Tony or Juan calling him to come back down, but the cry came from farther up the trail. He took the coat from his head but could not see through the hanging dust. He couldn't tell if the voice was calling for help. It was a high-pitched "woo-ooh" that turned into a "waah-aah," like a high singing, a chanting. The sound stopped abruptly. The wind kept up its own distinct siren.

He wanted to run back down the mountain. He got up, pulled his coat back over his head, and took a few steps down the trail. He stopped and listened as the wind subsided. The dust began to clear. It was completely quiet. To his right, miles away, he could see the tiny cars on Interstate 10 as they looped along the western edge of the Franklin Mountains. Johnny turned and squinted at the clear, white statue of Christ that towered above him.

He ran most of the rest of the way, over a mile of trail. The air was clear on the flat top of the mountain, as if the storm had never struck there. He paused, caught his breath, then looked over the edge and found Tony and Juan, two dots far below, still busy with their shovels. He moved toward the wooden stairs that rose to the monument, then stopped to drink from his canteen. He swallowed the cold water and listened. There was no wind.

Johnny climbed the stairs and knelt before the statue. He crossed himself, then rose to examine the fresh graffiti on the foundation. In bright blue spray paint someone had written "¡Venceremos O Nos Matan!" He knew it said something like "We shall overcome or be killed!" It was the first time he had seen any message like it on the statue and he was puzzled. The kind of words he usually found were "Gloria y Benny" or "Alicia does it with Dagoberto."

He set the can of whitewash on the ground and walked around the rectangular granite foundation without finding other signs of vandalism. As he came back to the side with the slogan, he saw a boy running down the wooden stairs.

"Hey! Come back here!" Johnny shouted. He raced after the boy, who leaped down the stairs, which resembled railroad tracks. The kid jumped over the last few steps and ran down the trail. Johnny followed. As they flew around a bend in the road, the boy slipped in the dirt and Johnny almost grabbed his shirt. When he reached for him again, the boy fell over the edge. Johnny slid to a stop on one knee and clung onto a large rock that protruded from the edge of the road. He watched the boy roll several yards and land in a cluster of cactus. If the sharp, stiff arms of the plants had not been there, he might have fallen another fifty feet.

"Ese, are you okay?" Johnny shouted. The boy lay still among the cactus. Johnny climbed down in a low squat and managed to get close enough to offer the boy his hand. "Vámonos arriba," Johnny told him and wrapped his arm around the stunned boy's shoulders.

"No! No!" the young, dirty face pleaded.

The boy was dressed in torn red jeans and a muddy yellow shirt. His bare feet were black with old dirt. Johnny stared at the boy's swollen soles and hardened calluses. He had never seen anyone out here without shoes. How could the boy get around the desert without cutting his feet to shreds? His face was the darkest brown Johnny had ever seen.

Johnny pulled himself up the cliff, bringing the boy, who did not struggle, with him.

"What were you doing?" Johnny asked when they were back on the level road. "Did you mess up the Cristo?"

"¿Qué?" the boy asked. He looked at Johnny's canteen on his belt. Johnny handed it to him.

"La pintura," Johnny answered. "¿Tú lo pintaste?"

The boy seemed too young to be painting political messages. Could he even spell? Even in Spanish?

"No," the boy said and handed the canteen back. His short black hair stood straight up. Parts of it were caked with mud. A couple of old scars angled across his forehead. His dark brown eyes gave Johnny a look he had never received from anyone.

"What's your name?" Johnny asked. "¿De dónde vienes?"

"Francisco. De Guatemala."

Johnny blinked. "¿Guatemala? ¿Vienes de Guatemala?" The boy could not have been more than nine or ten.

"Sí." Francisco looked over his shoulder at the desert below.

Johnny thought the boy wanted to run again. "¿Y tu familia?"

"En Juárez." The boy pointed south.

Johnny didn't know what to say. What was somebody from Guatemala doing up here? "Vente, Francisco."

He put his hand on the boy's shoulder, and Francisco cringed with pain. If he was hurt, Johnny needed to take him to Tony and Juan. They could drive him to the clinic in Sunland Park. But what then? If his family was in Juárez, would he try to get back to them? As an illegal, the boy had to dodge the Border Patrol.

They started down the mountain, Francisco walking with a slight limp. As they came around a bend, another dust storm twisted up the mountain. Johnny saw the brown clouds cover the road ahead. He thought of trying to walk through it to get Francisco down as fast as possible but was afraid he might lose him in the blinding dust.

The wind hit them with a shriek that sent stinging dirt and pebbles against their faces. Johnny motioned to Francisco to stop and led him to a low boulder beside the trail. They crouched down behind it. Johnny put his right arm around Francisco's shoulders and covered their heads with the jacket. Johnny smelled the heavy odor of sweat on the boy. The dust found them, stinging their bodies. Francisco hunched closer to Johnny. The storm shook the mountain and pushed curtains of sand against the two huddled figures. Johnny wondered if Tony and Juan were under cover. They had probably raised the canvas roof on the jeep and climbed inside. The dust storms never lasted long, but they could suffocate you with thick, dirty air. The two boys crouched lower against each other as the sand whistled into their legs and backs like dozens of pinpricks. They braced themselves against the spinning motion of the air as it traveled up the mountain. Johnny listened to the crazy wind and waited for it to move on.

Then he heard "Woo-ooh. Waa-aah." Francisco jumped as if shocked by an electric current. Johnny held him down as the storm mounted and the singing cut through the wind. He turned his lowered head to the terror in the kid's eyes.

"¡No! ¡No!" Francisco cried. "¡La mano blanca!"

A white hand? The cry seemed to come from above them, higher than the storm, but Johnny had seen no one else up there. He raised the coat a few inches to look at Francisco. The boy stared at him with watering eyes that glistened through the caked dirt on his face. They heard the cry again. "Wooh-aaah."

Johnny was about to say something to reassure Francisco when the dust hit harder, making them duck under the coat. As he bent lower to cover his head, Johnny felt a sharp kick in the ribs and the sting of dirt thrown in his face. Francisco kicked him again, bounded out of the coat, and ran up the trail into the dust. Johnny lay stunned on the ground, breathing hard, rubbing the burning dirt out of his eyes. He tried to sit up, but the pain and tears kept him lying there for several minutes. Finally, as the storm passed, he struggled to his feet. He wiped the sharp mix of tears and sand from his blinded eyes, stumbled, then waited to catch his breath and be able to see. He heard the sound of falling rocks above him.

Johnny started up the trail. The wind died. The air was clearing. He did not see the boy and figured he may have gone all the way to the cross. He hurried around a bend, hoping to see the fleeing figure, but there was no sign of him. As Johnny ran, he noticed how quiet everything had become. The air was clear, and the sun washed the statue with a brilliant white light.

Johnny ran up the steps to the monument and again walked

around the foundation. He did not see Francisco, but the can of whitewash that he had left on the ground, with the brush on top, was now open. The wet brush lay in the dirt beside it. On the south side of the monument he found the fresh writing: "Mi Dios." The white letters stood out neatly against the granite. They were not sloppy like typical graffiti. He heard a cough behind him and turned.

At the bottom of the stairs, an older boy stood behind the panting Francisco, both red in the face. The older boy was as dirty as Francisco and had scars on his forehead like Francisco's. His head had been shaved, the hair just starting to grow back.

Johnny took a step forward. The older boy held a small knife in the air, showing it to Johnny. Johnny stopped. The boy held Francisco tightly around the shoulders. Johnny wondered if they were brothers. The boy lowered the knife, his face sweating profusely. He wiped it on the sleeve of his dirty white T-shirt. He wore a pair of nearly new boots. His jeans were the same faded red as Francisco's. Johnny motioned to the canteen on his belt, wondering if they wanted water. The older boy shook his bald head and looked up at the cross. Francisco bowed his head as if ashamed.

Breaking the eerie silence, the sound of an approaching car startled all three of them. Francisco twisted out of the other boy's grip and ran up the stairs toward Johnny. The jeep with Tony and Juan came slowly up the road. Johnny stepped back as the older boy ran toward him so that he missed as he reached for Francisco, who ran past him and grabbed the open can of paint, then disappeared around the corner of the foundation. The older boy shoved Johnny hard against the wall. He hit it with a thud and went down, the pain in the back of his head spreading down his spine.

He sat there dizzily, rubbing the back of his head and moaning. Juan and Tony were going to be furious. As he struggled to his feet, he saw that the letters of "Mi Dios" were fading into the granite. The whitewash was so thin and watery it was being sucked into the dry wall.

Johnny went down the steps and looked over the edge. Juan and Tony had stopped the jeep on the last curve. They were filling several holes.

He climbed back to the cross and walked carefully around the walls. Both boys were gone. He stopped on the south side and rubbed the back of his head. The two boys were a hundred yards down the mountain, dust and tumbling rocks marking their hurried descent. They were headed toward Juárez. Francisco clutched the open can of whitewash in his right hand and followed his companion into a steep arroyo, where they disappeared.

Juan's and Tony's bobbing heads appeared at the crest of the road. "Mi Dios" had completely faded. But what about "Venceremos O Nos Matan"? He had to think of something to say about the missing can of paint. He couldn't think of anything as he waved to his brother and Juan from the top of the stairs. He thought he heard the wind and waited for the human cry to return and convince them that he had done nothing wrong.

Johnny turned his sore head south toward Juárez and saw the clouds of sand moving up the arroyos. The next phase of the storm was about to cover the monument with a fine and precious dust.

# FISHING

Roque took his son Martin fishing at an isolated spot on the Rio Grande. He chose the concrete bridge that spans the river at one of its deepest points north of El Paso. As he leaned against the railing, Roque looked up and down the asphalt road. It was an area with little traffic, an ideal spot. Roque watched as eleven-year-old Martin cast his line, which buzzed over their heads, then splashed into the water below. Roque saw that Martin remembered what he had taught the boy about casting.

He watched his son for a few minutes, then gazed at the Organ Mountains to the east. They seemed suddenly to move farther away, receding on the horizon. Roque tilted his baseball cap farther back on his head and sighed in contentment. Those distant peaks reminded him of his own father and how they used to fish in this area when Roque was a boy, long before the ugly bridge had been built.

This Saturday morning was special because it was Martin's birthday, and Martin skipped from one foot to the other with excitement until his father told him he would scare the fish. Martin settled down and imitated his father by leaning over the railing. As he peered down at the river, Martin felt something between them. He looked up to tears running down his father's whiskered face. His father wiped his eyes with his right hand and tilted his cap lower over his head. Martin gripped his fishing pole and asked his father what was wrong. Roque shook his head. Father and son stared across the water. Martin didn't know what to think. He moved several yards down and pulled the line along, wondering if this meant they would not be catching any fish today.

Roque let the slow tears run as a spray of dark clouds crashed into the jagged peaks of The Organs. The shadows of the clouds became dark hands that covered the ragged mountaintops until their rough outline vanished with the approaching change of sky. He thought of hands protecting the miles of unreachable mountains as if someone were keeping him from getting there to see their beauty from a closer point, holding him from feeling close to his son and the many things he wanted to tell him.

Roque and his son fished for almost two hours without a bite. They exchanged few words, each occupied with his own thoughts. Martin sat under the railing and dangled his legs over the side. Roque stood. A few cars went by. Neither of them paid attention to one that slowed as it passed them.

Martin shouted and started fighting his first fish. Roque wanted to guide him but let him do it himself. He could tell by the mild tug on the line that it was not going to be a big catch. Martin almost lost his cap as he lifted his arms over the railing, reeling in the small catfish. He waved the pole and kept the line clear until the catfish gave up. His father was surprised by how quickly the normally tough catfish quit fighting. He didn't tell his son that it was the tiniest catfish he had ever seen in these muddy waters. Martin held the hooked fish in the air for his father to see. It must have been only eight or nine inches, its long whiskers twitching defiantly. Martin's face beamed with pride under the shadow of his cap. Roque stared at his son and saw his own features in the smooth brown cheeks and deep green eyes.

Roque placed his hand on his son's and told him it was a good fish and that catching it was a good sign for the day. Martin's smile faded when more tears rolled down Roque's face. He didn't know how to ask his father why he was crying in the middle of their fun. Perhaps his father didn't really want to take him fishing on his birthday. This thought made Martin hurt inside. Roque let go of his son and stared toward a field thick with cotton beside the river. Roque was maneuvering his own line back toward his original spot when Martin tore the catfish off the hook and threw it over the railing.

Roque saw this out of the corner of his eye and turned as the fish hit the water. The late morning sun bounced blinding beams off the water. Roque studied the boy. Martin recast his line, his head bowed. Roque reeled in his line and set the pole against the railing. His son didn't know what was going to happen as his father embraced him. He almost dropped his pole as the man wrapped both arms around him. Roque burst into loud sobbing, repeating over and over that he loved Martin. The boy pulled his face back from his father's heaving chest and took a breath. His father had never done this before. What was going on? he wondered. He felt one of his father's tears land on his own face and asked why he was crying. Roque wiped the tears away, and they leaned against the railing. A flock of magpies rose out of the cottonwoods on the right bank, then disappeared beyond the first bend in the river.

Roque told Martin that when he was eleven years old, his father brought him to the river. They did not go fishing because his father wanted to show Roque where Tomas, his father's brother, had drowned. Roque pointed north and told Martin it was only four or five miles farther upriver. Tomas was an uncle Roque had never known. The year was 1939. Daniel, Roque's father, said Tomas had been running from the police in Juárez, Mexico. He had been falsely accused of robbing and murdering two members of a wealthy Juárez family, people he'd once worked for. Captured and tortured by the Juárez police, Tomas had escaped and gone into hiding in La Mesa, a town in La Mesilla Valley. He was planning to flee to Albuquerque when he drowned.

Roque told Martin that his grandfather brought him out here because Daniel wanted to tell his son that he thought Tomas was guilty. He'd reluctantly agreed to help Tomas when he called Daniel one night. Tomas had said he would wait for Daniel in La Mesa, but when Daniel drove there, he was told by two men that his brother was wandering like a madman up and down the river. Daniel searched along the river and spotted him on the opposite bank in the early morning. He yelled to Tomas to meet him at the first wooden bridge north of the town. Tomas waved back, acting drunk and crazy. In those days, Roque explained, the Rio Grande flowed deep and powerful and was more dangerous to cross than today. Daniel watched helplessly as his brother dove into the river, made it halfway across, then disappeared in the strong current. Daniel jumped in and almost drowned himself but could not reach Tomas. He barely made it back to shore.

Roque's father blamed himself for his brother's death. Daniel became obsessed with the Rio Grande. He would wander this area, get drunk, and stumble up and down the river, calling Tomas's name. Roque's mother left her husband and went back to Mexico. Roque never saw her again and didn't know where or how she died. Roque's father drank himself to death. Roque asked Martin if he recalled when his grandfather died. The boy, who'd been three years old at the time, shook his head.

Roque stopped talking when his line jerked. Martin jumped and gave a cry of joy. Roque strained to hold the line. An enormous catfish leaped from the water, then splashed down heavily. Martin shouted encouragement to his father, who managed a grin. He had not caught such a big catfish in years. It was fat and at least eighteen inches long. Roque fought it while Martin whooped and hollered.

As the two of them stood at the railing, Roque's pole bending high above them, a car approached slowly from the west side of the river. It had passed them earlier. Neither of them noticed it now until the sound of tires on asphalt caught their attention. Roque's grin vanished when he saw two men in the idling car staring at them. He stood firmly, splitting his attention between the straining line and the Mexican men. They sat in a beat-up Chevy, the door on the driver's side bashed in, the green paint revealing patches of rust. One of the men said something to the other and pointed at Roque.

"Hey, ese!" the driver said in a loud voice. "Catch anything?" He and the other man laughed. The fish finally gave up and came out of the water. Roque began to reel it in. He motioned to Martin to ignore the men and pull his line in. Martin scowled and did as his father told him. He broke down his pole as the man on the passenger side got out. Roque tried to grab the fish but couldn't reach it. It kept twisting beyond the railing. He let his heavy catch hang below as he faced the man.

"Ese," the passenger started, "let's have your fish. We're hungry." He stopped in the middle of the road.

Martin shook his head defiantly and moved closer to his father. Roque yanked on his pole to pull his fish over the railing. But he was distracted by the intruder, and the pole slipped from his hands and fell with a clatter on the asphalt. The fish, still beyond the railing, hovered in the air for a second. Sunlight radiated off its smooth body as it fell from the broken line. Roque, Martin, and the stranger froze as the fish dropped into the river with a tremendous splash.

Roque charged toward the stranger, fists clenched, but the younger man ran to the car. The driver gunned the engine with a thunderous roar as his partner jumped in. Roque picked up a couple of rocks and threw them at the fleeing car. One of them bounced off the side. As the car crossed the bridge, the driver stuck an arm out and gave Roque the finger.

Martin watched the whole thing, then picked up both fishing poles. His father motioned to him that it was time to leave. They gathered their gear, and Martin followed his father's brisk walk to their car. Roque opened the trunk, and they dropped the poles and tackle box inside. He slammed it shut, unlocked the doors, and sat behind the steering wheel, staring straight ahead. Martin was afraid to make a sound. Finally, he started the car and headed for La Mesa.

Martin had never been in the town, and the sight of so many crumbling adobe houses made him forget the fish momentarily. He saw stray dogs crossing the highway and a few people standing in front of the lone grocery store. They passed quickly through La Mesa in silence.

They came to a railroad crossing and Roque stopped. He lowered his window. He recognized the row of cottonwoods that grew parallel to the tracks. He drove across the tracks and turned onto a dirt road. Roque maneuvered the car onto a levee road barely wide enough for the vehicle. They drove along the levee, paralleling the cement irrigation channel, until they came to a metal gate across their path. Roque motioned to his son to open the gate. Martin got out and lifted the bars, then stood aside as Roque drove through. The boy closed the gate and climbed back into the car. As he sat back, he smelled fish on his hands. He stared at his father as the car bounced over the bumpy path. Its bottom smashed against the hard surface a couple of times. Finally, Roque turned the steering wheel and let the car roll down the end slope of the levee. He stopped twenty yards from the river.

Roque told his son that this was the place. Martin didn't know what he was talking about. He stayed in the car while his father got out. This infuriated Roque, who came to the passenger side, yanked the door open, bent down, and whispered into Martin's ear that this was the site of Tomas's drowning. He grabbed his son roughly by the shoulder and pulled him out. Roque realized what he was doing and released his grip on Martin. He patted his son on the head and led him toward the water. They walked along the bank, thick cattails and saltcedars making it difficult to get close to the river. Martin wondered how his father knew that this was the place after so many years. As they struggled over the prickly terrain, Martin kept an eye out for the men who made his father lose his fish. He expected their car to appear on the levee, any second.

Roque paused under a cottonwood whose enormous bent fork grew over the water. He nodded to himself, then turned to the boy. He told Martin this was the old tree where Daniel had tried to save Tomas, how he climbed out on it in a desperate attempt to grab his brother. The river here seemed muddier and darker than where they had been fishing. When Roque's tears came this time, Martin was not surprised.

Roque took off his cap to wipe his face. Martin asked how he knew this was the tree. It was the wrong thing to ask. His father gave a low grunt and jumped into the river. Martin screamed. Roque landed in a shallow pool of mud. He splashed it on both of them, then Roque slipped once, fell under, and came up completely covered. Martin laughed. Roque headed toward the deeper water but got stuck in the mud, which rose above his knees. He thought about the last time he'd seen his father alive in the hospital, dying at the age of sixty-two. Daniel had opened his eyes and gripped his son by the collar. Roque had leaned down and smelled death. Daniel had whispered, "Don't forget it is the river." He died three days later.

Roque heard his father's voice now and started to climb toward his son. He slipped and needed Martin's help to get out.

They fell back onto dry grass. Martin couldn't stop laughing as they rolled on the ground. His father's muddy face was one of the funniest things he had ever seen. Roque sat up, wiped his face with his dirty hands, and also laughed. He grabbed Martin and held on tight as they laughed and laughed, these moments burning in Roque's stomach. They made Martin love and hate his father for the years to come.

Part Three

# TRAIN STATION

I waited for him in the old train station in El Paso, a place I rarely entered in the twenty-five years I lived there. The enormous building was nearly deserted, even though the train from San Antonio had just pulled in. The long corridors and high ceilings amplified the footsteps of every person that walked across the ancient marble floors. I sat on a long wooden bench and waited for him to get off the train. I don't know why I didn't meet him at the train, where the passengers got off. I watched several people enter through the swinging doors that led to the trains. As I waited, an old Mexican woman came through the doors. She carried what looked like a small duffle bag in her arms and had a worried expression on her face. She looked like she had been traveling for a long time. Her wrinkled face and wild white hair reminded me that I might not recognize him as he came through the doors. How old was he? How much had my mother really told me about him? I tried to recall the last clear photograph of him that she had shown me as a boy. It may have been the one where he is standing in front of his 1929 Ford, his overalls holding up his huge belly, the cowboy hat hiding his eyes in shadows as he stares grimly into the camera.

I got up, expecting him to come through the doors, but no one appeared. Why couldn't I have met him at the train after all this time, instead of allowing my shy hesitation to keep me on the bench? I hoped we would recognize each other, embrace awkwardly, and try to say something to close the years between us. After all, my mother told me that he has wanted to see me for many years. I wanted him to walk through those doors and find me right away, tell me how Arizona had been all these years, recount stories about the family that no one had told me. It couldn't be that hard to find each other. I was the only one waiting in the cavernous train station. I listened to the footsteps of the last arriving passengers and waited as their echoes faded down the hallways leading to the street. When the station was quiet again, I rose. I understood that he was going to be the last one off the train.

I walked across the empty room and went through the swinging doors to the gates. Through the glass windows I saw that the walls of the corridor were decorated like a museum. Dozens of old black-and-white photographs hung on each wall, the story of the historic station and the history of El Paso. I passed through the doors and paused before the first row of photographs. From where I stood, I could see the train outside. Not a single person was in sight. I walked to the end of the corridor, stepped into the hot air outside, and looked up and down the length of the tracks and the trains. I saw no one.

I turned around, thinking I might have missed him as he came through the doors. He might be inside the station, perhaps having stopped in the men's room. In her letter my mother said he would be on this train because it was the one the railroad allowed their people to ride. Before going back inside, I stopped in front of a wide 1938 photograph of a railroad crew. The men stood in front of the train. Some sat atop a tiny flatcar used for transporting crews to repair the tracks or lay new line. I stared at the photo and recognized him right away.

He sat on the flatcar, his big belly bulging against those familiar overalls. His round, dark face smiled under the huge Mexican cowboy hat. Was it the same hat I recalled from that other photograph? He held a cigarette in his right hand, the left propped on his knee. He did not smile as brightly as the other men in his crew. The moustache was a detail I did not remember from the photographs I'd gazed at years ago. He had been here in the station the whole time, framed inside this eternal moment. Did he know his image was here?

As I looked at the photo again, one of the station guards came up to me. "No more trains tonight," he muttered and looked at his watch. "This was the last one."

I nodded, took a few steps past him, then stopped. "You didn't happen to see an old man in a cowboy hat get off this train, did you?" I asked.

He shook his head. "But there was an elderly man with a hat on the previous train. I remember him because of his big black moustache. That was over an hour ago."

I nodded. I was tempted to look at the photo one more time but walked away. Had he arrived earlier than planned? Was my mother's letter wrong? Was he out on the street somewhere? As I passed through the swinging doors, I was sure he had been on the earlier train.

I paused, then decided to take one more look at the photographs. I headed back to the display, my hurried footsteps booming across the cavernous place. Before studying them again, I made sure no one was watching me. I focused on the photo of the railroad crew. He gazed into the camera with a mixture of defiance and pride. I saw the resemblances in his wide cheekbones, and the eyes that told me there were many things about the family that he could tell me. His face was the face of a man who'd worked hard for many years, but it was also that of someone who knew he belonged elsewhere.

I thought about the restlessness he displayed in the photo-graph as I retreated to the waiting room. I listened to the last echoes of my footsteps on the marble floors. My mother's letter said he was coming to explain why he had stayed away for so many years and why his life in Arizona had been kept from my sisters and me for so long.

I headed toward my car. As I emerged into the empty lot, the sound of traffic from downtown hovered over the quieter atmo-sphere of the station. I looked toward the tall buildings and knew he was already here but had left the station without waiting for me. Perhaps he had spotted the photograph and was embarrassed. I got in my car, drove out of the lot, and noticed a couple of men walking down the street toward the Paso del Norte, the hotel closest to the station. My mother had once written that he loved to stay there when he visited. I pulled into the valet parking, took the ticket from the attendant, and ran into the hotel. The sound of clinking glasses and jazz music filled the brightly decorated lobby. I walked to the counter and asked the clerk if a Bonifacio Canales had checked in.

"Let me look it up for you," the young guy said.

I scanned the lobby full of people.

"Yes, we have a Mr. Canales. He is one of our regular ten-ants."

"What do you mean?"

The clerk looked surprised. "Mr. Canales has been living here for many years."

I stared at him. "His room number?"

The clerk gave it to me. I went to the house phone and dialed. After three rings he answered. "Sí?"

"Grandpa?" I asked, my voice trembling.

"Mijo? Is it you?"

"Yes, Grandpa. I was supposed to pick you up at the station.

I didn't know you came in on a different train. I didn't know you were here. How long have you lived here without telling me?"

He coughed. "Come up to my room."

He hung up before I could say anything else. I was stunned. No one had told me my grandfather was living in El Paso's most elegant and historic hotel. I couldn't believe he had been hiding in this place, living a secret life that my mother kept from her children. But did she know? I always believed her letters. It was only recently, when I had been doing research in the city library, that I found a book about Yaqui railroad workers in Arizona. His name was mentioned several times in chapters about families migrating from northern Mexico to Arizona at the turn of the century. He had been one of the community leaders who helped many Yaqui men get work on the railroads. When I called my mother to tell her about the book, it was the first time she'd acknowledged that he was still alive. When I asked why she'd told me that he had died forty years ago, there was silence on the other end. Days later, she called to tell me he was coming to visit and talk to me about our family.

I took the elevator to the fourth floor, hurried down the richly carpeted hallway, and found room 412. I knocked and the door opened slowly. Bonifacio Canales, my grandfather, stood there dressed in the same faded overalls, dusty work boots, and wide hat he wore in the photographs. His armpits were damp with heavy sweat stains, and his face was a very dark brown. The large moustache dominated his features.

"Mijo," my grandfather beckoned. A smell I recognized from the train station drifted into the hallway.

"Mijo," he whispered and raised both arms in welcome. I entered the room and closed the door behind us.

# THE GHOST OF JOHN WAYNE

Tony Marin read about it in the *San Antonio Light* Sunday magazine and couldn't believe it. A reporter had hired a local psychic to find out if the ghost of John Wayne was haunting the Alamo. For years it had been a local joke that John Wayne's ghost couldn't stay away from the beloved shrine that was the basis for his movie of the famous battle. Somebody at the newspaper must have decided to pull this stunt for a story, Tony thought as he read the article. Wandering around the tourist-crowded shrine in the middle of downtown San Antonio, the psychic had discovered the restless spirits of two Mexican soldiers. He was able to communicate with one, who told him that the ghost of John Wayne came to the Alamo every now and then but never spoke with the soldiers. He would drift in and out of the tiny chapel, then disappear. The psychic told the *Light* reporter that the soldiers were brothers, Jose and Anselmo Vargas, who'd been conscripted into General Santa Ana's army and had died together in the battle. Their spirits, said the psychic, are trapped in one of the rooms of the chapel. They cannot find eternal peace because of the way they had died.

Tony reread the article, amazed at the reporter's seriousness in writing about a Hollywood actor haunting a Texas shrine. Did people really believe this? After reading the story a third time, Tony decided the psychic, Bill Benson, was telling the truth about making contact with the spirits of the Mexican soldiers. He wondered how many hundreds of souls were trapped forever under the endless lines of tourists who came from all over the world to see the Alamo. That part of the story he could believe. He had read enough about Santa Ana and the Mexican army to know that thousands of young men were forced to join and die for the dictator's dreams of glory. Tony wondered what deeper darkness the Texan defenders of the Alamo carried to their graves.

He read the article a fourth time and was finally convinced, though he knew nothing about psychic phenomena and had never encountered ghosts or spirits. Two days later, he looked up Bill Benson in the phone book and called him. An answering machine took his message. Tony wondered if Benson had received many calls about the article. He decided to go to the Alamo, a place he had not visited in years. What he disliked most was the Texas Ranger at the door whose job was to make sure no one entered with a hat on.

Sure enough, the Ranger was there. "Please remove your hat. Please remove your hat." No man or woman was going to violate the sanctity of the place. Tony watched the line of tourists move slowly into the chapel and get in step.

The line moved closer to the wooden doors of the chapel, and he entered the cool interior of the Alamo. For a moment it reminded him of his childhood days of going to church with his mother and abuela every Sunday, but the Alamo had been stripped of its religious mood long ago, the main chapel transformed into a museum of artifacts and mementos from the battle —a monument to Texas nationalism. He walked around the crowded room and inspected the glass cases that contained old rifles, flags, and what was claimed to be Jim Bowie's famous knife. He spent several minutes studying the intricate miniature replica of the 1836 mission and the surrounding walls. Many of the barricades and buildings were now gone, long replaced by paved streets, a post office, a McDonald's, and a Ripley's Believe It Or

Not Museum—downtown San Antonio crowding the mission from all directions.

Tony stopped at one of the tiny rooms off the left side of the chapel, cell-like chambers closed to the public by black bars across the arched doorways. Benson had told the reporter that he had made contact with the spirits of the Mexican soldiers in one of these rooms, where many had died in the battle. The spirits, according to Benson, said John Wayne's ghost would stand in the doorway and stare at the trapped men. They never felt threatened by Wayne, who looked at them without a word. Tony wondered if Wayne was checking the Mexicans to see if they were authentic enough for casting in his movie. How did these Mexicans of 1836 even know who John Wayne was?

Tony snickered as more people crowded around him. As he stared at the brick walls of the cells, he was pushed by an elderly woman who lodged herself next to him to get a better view. He moved aside when she grabbed the vertical bars and pushed her face against them. She peered intently into the empty chamber. Tony turned to a plaque on the floor that marked the spot where several human bones had been uncovered in 1920. He wondered why only one spot had been singled out when this whole floor must cover thousands of remains.

He felt a chill and left the chapel by the exit at the left rear. He cut through another line of people who were entering the museum shop in the next building, where The Daughters of the Republic of Texas made sure you left a donation to the cause by buying Alamo T-shirts, hats, mugs, books, posters, and other items. He didn't go inside but sat under the huge tree in the courtyard, an ancient cottonwood whose massive black limbs reached high above the passing tourists. He watched people come and go and wondered why he'd called Benson.

Tony went home and forgot about his visit to the Alamo. One

night, three weeks later, while he was working at his desk, the phone rang. It was Benson.

"Oh, yes," Tony perked up, surprised. "I tried to get ahold of you after the article on the Alamo came out. I thought you might be busy or didn't want calls about the article."

"You are the only one who called," Benson said in a calm voice.

"Really? I thought you'd get a lot of people wanting to find out more about John Wayne's spirit."

"John Wayne's ghost," Benson corrected him.

"Ghost? What's the difference?"

Tony reached for a notebook and pen.

"The spirits of the Mexican soldiers are in the Alamo," Benson explained. "But when I encountered them, they said it is the ghost of John Wayne that comes around, not his spirit. His ghost appears in a neutral state with no sense of being trapped or of wanting to resolve his state so he can go on. The Mexican spirits are trapped. They want out of there, to be laid to rest. Ghosts are usually satisfied with their neutral state even if they are bothering you by appearing. Spirits want to transform themselves toward . . ."

Tony waited. "Toward what?"

"I don't know," Benson said quickly. "I'm not even sure why I am telling you this. Are you a reporter, too?"

"I'm a writer, not a reporter. I teach at San Antonio College. I'm working on a book of essays about Texas, and I hoped you could tell me more about the Alamo."

"Isn't the story enough, or do you think it's all phony and I must be crazy?"

Tony heard the defensiveness in Benson's voice. "No, I don't think you're crazy. I wouldn't have tried to reach you if I did."

"I think the reason people didn't call is that they found it sacrilegious that John Wayne would come around to such a holy place." His sarcasm made Tony feel at ease.

"I'm surprised you didn't get threats from The Daughters of the Republic of Texas," Tony said. Benson laughed for the first time. "Actually, I think they're delighted that John Wayne would haunt the Alamo. They're probably upset over the idea that Mexican spirits are still inside their place. It's probably the purists who sent me the letter."

"What letter?" Tony stopped taking notes.

Benson was silent for several seconds. "We haven't met. I need to get back to work. I can't talk anymore."

"Why did you return my call?" Tony asked carefully, trying to keep him on the line. "Can we meet?"

Benson didn't hesitate. "Okay. I'm free tomorrow at two. Where would you like to meet?"

"The flower garden behind the Alamo."

"How will I know you?"

Tony described himself. "I'll recognize you by your picture in the paper."

"Tomorrow at two." Benson hung up.

TONY SAT in the lush garden behind the Alamo as several dozen people wandered around the landscaped plots of bluebonnets, gardenias, roses, and other bright flowers. Several of the tourists stood over the *acequia* and watched the huge orange and white fish that swam in it. He took in the peaceful scene and wondered what lay beneath the healthy green grass and the attractive acres within the ancient walls.

He recognized Benson right away but was surprised at how thin and meek he looked. Benson was middle-aged, with a balding head. He wore a white tennis shirt and faded Levis. He looked like a retired professor.

Tony rose, and they shook hands. Benson carried a large manila envelope in his left hand.

They sat on the bench by the Coke machines near the bathrooms, not the quietest place in the compound to talk. "Should we walk around?" Tony started to rise.

"No, this is fine." Benson squinted and placed sunglasses on his pale face.

"Thanks for agreeing to meet. Do you get a lot of demands on your time?"

"Not really."

Benson looked out across the peaceful gardens. "I don't do much of this anymore."

"Much of what?"

"Find ghosts."

"I thought you said spirits on the phone."

Benson looked at Tony. "I used to make good money helping the police find missing persons. That kind of work was easier than this."

"Does it bother you to come here?"

"Yes." Benson looked around to see if anyone was listening.

"Why did you agree to do it for the *Light* reporter?"

"They paid good money. They wanted a story."

Tony looked toward the chapel and thought about what Benson had said in the article. He'd told the reporter he couldn't stay inside the mission long because there were too many trapped spirits pushing at him.

"I don't have any money to offer you, but I was wondering if you could tell me or, I guess, *show* me the spirits of the soldiers."

Tony felt uncomfortable asking this.

Benson's eyebrows rose. "You mean you don't want to find John Wayne?"

"I don't care about John Wayne. I want to know about the brothers who died in the battle."

"Don't you believe me about John Wayne? If you read the article carefully, the Mexicans acknowledge contact with Wayne. I didn't find him when I went in there."

"I read it carefully," Tony said.

"Not everyone did." Benson waved the envelope in his hand.

"What's that?"

"A letter I got after the article came out. I was rather surprised at the lack of mail on this one. But this letter is rather interesting. Texas, I guess."

He handed the envelope to Tony, who opened it and read the scratchy handwriting. "You are a lunatic to say those things about the Alamo. You are crazy to insult us by saying those dumb Mexicans are in there. John Wayne was right. Don't ever talk about the Alamo like that in public, or we are going to haunt you ourselves." There was no signature.

"Have you contacted the police?" Tony handed the letter back.

"No," Benson laughed. "They won't pay attention to threats against me. They're used to people reacting like this."

"Are you scared? Who do you think wrote this?"

"I don't know."

Benson shrugged and placed the letter back in the envelope. "A Texas history buff. Who knows?"

Tony looked around, apprehensive for the first time since their phone conversation.

"So, why do you want to make contact with the Mexican soldiers?" asked Benson.

"I don't know if contact is what I want," Tony tried to explain. "I just need to know if there's a better way to understand the meaning of this place."

Benson sat up straight. "Look around you. People come here, stand in line, buy Davy Crockett coffee cups, and smell these flowers. I think we *have* come to terms with what this place means to millions of people."

Tony smiled. "You know there's more to it than that."

Benson stood slowly. "Yeah, I've always found there's more to everything."

"Are we going inside?"

"This is a good time of day. It's not as crowded in the afternoon."

Tony's brief excitement turned to fear. What would he do if Benson made contact with whoever was inside the Alamo? They walked through the quiet gardens and passed a Japanese couple giggling and shooting pictures of each other among the flowers. As they approached the chapel, Benson slowed his walk, his shoulders drooping lower on his thin frame. A twitch appeared beneath his left eye. His cheeks turned a slight red. The entry line was not long, and they were inside in ten minutes. As soon as they entered, Benson folded his arms over his chest and walked carefully, as if he didn't want to touch anything. They walked around the museum, neither one saying a word. They stood in front of the table that held the miniature replica of the original mission and fort compound, tiny toy soldiers enclosed in the glass. Tony stared at the display, though he'd seen it before.

Three tourists wandered over to the exhibit, and Benson quickly stepped away from them. He went to one of the tiny cells that lined the walls, put a hand on one of the black iron bars, and peered inside. Tony watched the trancelike glaze come over Benson's eyes. He stood a few feet away and hoped people wouldn't crowd Benson, who leaned against the bars, resting his forehead against them.

Tony looked behind him and spotted the Texas Ranger making his rounds. He turned back to Benson and saw terror on the man's face. Benson's cheeks sucked inward. He closed his eyes. His bits of gray hair stood out for a second, as if someone were combing it. Now Benson opened his eyes wide, whispered something that Tony couldn't hear, then turned and walked out the back exit. Tony hurried after him, pushing aside a young kid who blocked the door. "Sorry," he muttered, and ran after Benson, who was heading toward the bench in the garden.

Benson sat down, his chest heaving, his breath short and raspy. He rested his head in his hands, elbows on his knees.

"Are you alright?" Tony asked as he sat next to him.

"I'll be okay," Benson answered. "Let me get a drink of water."

Tony waited as Benson went to the fountain near the bathrooms, then came back. They sat in silence for several minutes. People streamed out of the Alamo and into the tourist shop, the afternoon starting to draw more visitors.

"Can you talk?" Tony asked, finally.

"Yes."

"What happened?"

"I found others I didn't see the first time."

"The brothers?"

"They weren't there. It is rare to encounter the same spirits twice. They were other Mexican soldiers, all very young. They're trapped in there—sixty or seventy who fell in that room during the battle."

Tony didn't know what to say.

"I was surprised I heard so many voices. It was as if they knew that someone like me had been there recently. It was too much." He sighed. "But I need to go back in there. Someone showed me something."

"What was it?"

"I'm not sure I can say. There was too much agony, voices crying out. One of them wanted to show me something. I need to find out what it is."

Tony saw a man twenty feet away, near a bed of bluebonnets. He was standing still and staring at them. Tony lowered his head. "Don't look up. There's a man watching us. Over there by those bluebonnets."

Benson sat back casually and scanned the garden. "What about him? Are you getting paranoid?"

"He's watching us."

"So? There are lots of strange people downtown, and some of them come here."

"Do you want me to go in with you?"

"Of course."

Tony followed Benson to the end of the line, and soon they were inside again. Benson took his time moving to the cell where he'd been overcome. They strolled around the museum, studied the Bowie knives in the case, and finally found themselves near the barred room. Benson stopped a few feet in front of the bars, unable to get closer because people blocked his way. An elderly couple and their three grandchildren were peering into the cell, the awe on their faces a common expression among visitors. Benson waited patiently and closed his eyes, his arms folded over his chest. Tony saw the man he'd seen outside. Leaning against one of the display cases, he was staring at Benson. When the tourists moved away from the bars, Benson took their place and placed his hands on the iron. Tony moved back to keep a better eye on the man who was watching. He saw a tiny ID badge on the man's shirt. The fellow was Benson's age and wore a white short-sleeved shirt and black jeans. His hair was in a crew cut.

Tony heard a low moan and turned to look. Benson was gripping the bars and staring intently into the room, where the only thing Tony saw was a Texas flag. Benson muttered to himself, let go of the bars, and kept looking in, the shock gone from his face. Then he turned and waved Tony closer.

"The two brothers," he whispered. "They're back."

"What?" Tony whispered.

"They want to be released. They showed me what I thought I saw earlier." Sweat ran down Benson's pale forehead.

"Are you okay?"

"There is something here besides the spirits of the dead."

Benson wasn't moving. His eyes were closed. The man who'd been watching them was talking to one of the Texas Rangers. The two of them kept looking in Tony and Benson's direction.

As the Ranger walked toward them, Tony asked Benson, "What do you see? I need to know." His anxiety made him dizzy.

"There's a flag in there."

"Yeah, the Texas flag. So what?" The Ranger's approach was blocked by people, some asking him questions.

"No," Benson answered. "There's another flag in there, draped around the body of one of the Vargas brothers. His brother has been trying to pull it off. It's a white flag."

"The Texans tried to surrender?" Tony was startled.

"I don't know. The brother is trying to say something. He keeps pulling the white flag from his brother's body but can't free it. I can't see. Too much smoke. Cries. Too many dead. The brother is saying they were given the white flag. It belongs to them. They thought the battle was over, but they were all killed. The white flag."

"It belongs to the Mexican soldiers?" Tony was confused. The Texas Ranger was ten feet away.

"Yes, I think so, but it was given to them. I can't see clearly. I think many of them died trying to stop the battle."

"Surrendering?" Tony pleaded. "Who was surrendering? Who gave them the flag?"

The Ranger stopped behind them. He was a tall man with a stone face and crew cut, the stereotype of a Texas Ranger. "You folks need to keep moving along. We have many people who want to see the exhibits."

Benson blinked, sweat dripping off his nose. He wiped it with his hand and started to leave. Tony was glad the Ranger didn't ask questions. The man who'd watched them in the gardens was listening, a few feet away. Tony and Benson went outside, walked through the gardens awhile, then sat. The man who'd watched them came toward them.

"That's him," Tony said. "He put the Texas Ranger on us."

"What?" Benson was still trying to recover.

The husky man was upon them. "I know you!" he shouted at Benson.

Tony jumped up. "What are you doing?"

"You're the weirdo in the paper who said Mexicans are in there!" the guy hissed.

Benson looked at the man.

"Why don't you go away." Tony stood his ground.

The guy pushed Tony down onto the bench. Benson didn't react, just bowed his head.

"You weirdos are always trying to get in the paper. I'm telling you, we aren't going to put up with that crap about Mexicans in there!" The man pointed a pudgy finger at Benson, then walked away, unconcerned that Tony had risen with fists clenched.

"Don't," Benson said. "Let him go."

Tony swayed, his face red, his heart pounding. Tourists in the garden stared at them, then kept moving. Tony sat down with a sigh. The man disappeared into the crowd.

"Damn nut," said Tony.

"I've encountered people like him before," Benson replied.

"I wanted to hit him."

Benson shook his head. "It always comes to that. But the truth is, none of us knows what truly happened in there. What I saw today? It's not going to change anything. The spirits will be locked in there forever."

"What about the white flag? What does it mean?"

"We're not supposed to know who waved the flag, who was trying to surrender. It would change history, and people don't want that."

They sat quietly, then walked through the gardens and out onto Alamo Street, where they paused in front of the huge marble monument erected in honor of the Texas defenders.

"Thanks for doing this."

Tony shook Benson's cold hand. "You have been a great help."

"Thank you for being so patient," Benson said. He turned and crossed the street without looking back.

Tony started to walk to his car. He was feeling sad. Waiting for a traffic light to turn green, he decided to return to the Alamo. He entered the gift shop next to the mission. The store was packed with people. It featured everything that could make money for the Alamo—Davy Crockett caps, Sam Houston T-shirts, rubber Bowie knives for the kids, even a section of books on Texas history. The lines at the cash registers were long. He jostled his way through the crowd to the book section. Hundreds of books on the battle and its heroes lined the shelves. He scanned the titles on the spines until he found one on the history of Alamo films.

Tony stood in line to pay. He couldn't see clearly over the heads in front of him until he drew closer to the registers. When only three customers remained between him and the counter, he spotted what he was looking for. He pulled out his checkbook, struggling to keep a straight face. When it was his turn, he set the book down hard on the glass counter. The clerk looked up and recognized him, but there were too many people around for either one to acknowledge their earlier encounter. The man rang up the book and stared while Tony wrote the check and slipped it across the glass without handing it to him.

"Driver's license," the man hissed.

Tony pulled it out of his wallet. Would the man track him down this way? It didn't matter. The man wrote the license information on the back of the check. As Tony picked up his license and the book, the man backed away from the counter and whispered something to the woman clerk next to him. They watched Tony leave, the smile on his face about to break into a nervous quiver. He gave them a nod and walked out.

# AWAY

He tries to find his way back to his truck. In his mescal up-
heaval, he staggers and takes the wrong Juárez street. He is lost
in the town that has fascinated him for years, a place that spills
its garbage and its poor people across the river. A fading blue
streetlight casts shadows over the trees that line the sidewalk.
They are planted into the cement and make him wonder how
they grow through the concrete. He staggers again, wonders if
it will be a familiar street that leads him back to the bridge. He
walks through a neighborhood of tiny cubicles, every apartment
door the same as the last, rows of buildings falling down, walls
ripped, burned, painted over many times. The walls of Juárez are
not covered with graffiti like in El Paso. He counts the curtains
and dirty cloths that hang from the screen doors, hiding one- and
two-room dwellings, poverty that continues to fascinate him. The
clear night flickers around the dull glow of El Paso's city lights to
the north, the three red beacons on Mount Franklin blinking and
locking him into a spinning trance his feet are used to, the walk of
someone who has not crossed the bridge to visit in several years.
The weary mescal haze blows him down the dirt streets as if he'd
never left his hometown.

As he turns a corner, two men are leaning against a car. They
watch silently as he goes past. One whispers something to the
other, but he can't tell what the Spanish is. For a moment they
look as if they are going to come after him. One wears a dirty New

York Yankees baseball cap and is covered with oil and dirt, as if he just got off work at a garage. The other wears an old leather jacket despite the heat. This one holds out an arm as he walks past. The hand is covered with tattoos, the fingers blue and green. The heads of the two men fuse together as he takes another hesitant step. Their dark Mexican skin seeps into the shadows in a beauty he has missed, the signal that good and bad things become acts of disappearance. As he moves on, they become the blackness of the border, a quick act of magic that he must keep to himself if he is to find the bridge back to El Paso.

He senses danger and slows down. Dozens of lamps and electric lights come on at the same instant, the muddy streets sinking in the darkness, laundry suds floating down the gutters, miniature explosions inside their bubbles reminding him he is lost, the colonia the same barrio across the river where he grew up. As he staggers on, he recalls a broken area of wire and wooden fences, small porches in front of identical houses, all the same except the large blue home of his grandmother—the lone house he always finds when he drives through the barrio of his birth north of the freeway. Each time he returns, the house is standing there, part of the three blocks spared the progress of a growing city that wiped out dozens of square miles of his neighborhood to build the only freeway in El Paso, the wide road that reminds him he is lost on the other side.

He hears whispers behind him and turns. The men are not there. He hurries down the street, knowing he is close to the bridge. Then laughter in the air, the sound of a toilet flushing, and the cry of a small child. Broken bottles and beer cans flash on the ground. He passes a dark alley where an old woman lies on a piece of cardboard. She is asleep, her arms tucked under her head, which is wrapped in a dirty scarf. Her brown dress is torn, but she wears something thicker underneath. An empty wicker basket sits near her head. The bony knuckles on her folded hands glisten in the dark. He pauses to take a second look and sees a rosary bunched under her chest. He crosses the street and stops in front of a portable stove burner on wheels. A middle-aged man stands frying and selling paper plates of gorditas, tripitas, and tacos. The stand is only twenty yards from the alley, and he suspects that the beggar woman has not eaten. Why has she chosen to sleep so close to the aroma of frying food? The man works beneath a striped canopy with bright lights over the smoking stove, crying out, "Taquitos! Gorditas!"

The smell of the food makes him feel like throwing up, but he can never heave the longing from his stomach. He has to take the smell with him and find the sleeping woman in the alley, eating a steamy plate of tripitas he will buy for her.

He turns down the next corner toward the lights of Avenida Juárez, the first street he recognizes, and passes a row of shops, their windows jammed with toy dolls, cars, clothing, jigsaw puzzles, magazines with naked women on the covers, glass decorations, and masks. One large window reflects the colors of the paper kites hanging from every inch of ceiling inside. There is even a kite with the face of Elvis on it. A fat ballerina is imprinted on another, the enormous smile on her face spanning the width of the kite, as if its maker thought a distorted dancer would be attractive to kite buyers. Suddenly, he sees the kite that takes him to Denver, where he lived for twelve years. He can't believe it. The bright red face of an Indian glowers at him from the ceiling. It is the face of the mad poet in Denver who disrupted readings all over town. He was notorious for appearing with his face painted red and telling audiences that it was his poetry mask and he could not read without it. He did not just slash red lines across his cheeks and nose but completely covered his face in a thick layer of red. It was him on the kite hanging in the back corner. He could see it clearly through the window. A car goes by, and he begins walking again, feeling the stares of the wooden and plastic faces from the shop window.

In his thirst and mescal burping, he can't miss what appears next. It stops him in his tracks and makes him sway in the heat of the night, a smell of sweat he notices for the first time. He stares in drunken amazement at the arrangement of portraits and paintings mounted on a rectangular board in the window of the next shop. The painting that holds him is of a woman in dark blue robes. She floats over a stone bridge, beneath which enormous orange flames twist down the surface of the river. The heads of fish, other women, and screaming men bob in the water. The background is a combination of black and purples that rise in a deep night sky inhabited by round creatures with faces of bearded men. Razor-sharp stars cascade from the men's eyes onto the floating woman. One star on the top right corner of the canvas shines like a heavenly shield of armor. He strains through the glass until he finds what resembles a totem pole orbiting on the top left corner of the painting. It is a narrow cylinder with primitive brown faces on it. It is painted at the farthest point on the canvas from the woman in robes. He thinks of Max Ernst, the surrealist painter who wandered in Mexico and settled in Arizona in the forties. This artist must know Ernst's work. He thinks of this because of the strange European woman he had drunk with in a bar in Juárez the day before. All she talked about was finding the wild artists who fled Europe for Mexico. She was very drunk and told him she once knew Max Ernst, could show him where four unknown Ernst paintings were hidden in a villa in Juárez. He'd laughed at her and reeled out of the bar.

A second painting, larger than the first, is of a garden of beautiful yet distorted flowers and trees. The central point is a tree of triangular green leaves spreading outward in circular patterns. In each pattern the faces of bald men scream in detailed agony, their purple skin darker than that of the pedestrians passing behind him as he leans on the glass of the storefront. They move quietly, distract him momentarily. He continues to look through the window. Around the tree of purple faces, thick patches of blue and yellow flowers rise to surround and protect the suffering men.

The third painting visible through the glass is a small, rectangular canvas. A man kneels among tall grass and slithering vines that spill over the borders of the painting. The man is naked except for a loincloth, his long black hair standing in the air as if electrified, his arms clutching the thick vines as he tries to pull them out of the ground.

He can't see any more paintings, but he'll return, if he can find this street when sober. The sign above the door says Icarro's Galleria. He tries the door. It's locked. His stomach begins to pull him away, the dizzy sidewalk giving him its own designs.

He trips and falls to one knee and laughs, the churning mescal dulling the pain. As he gets up, he touches the bulge in his right pocket, a rosary that a drunk had given him in the cantina. He hears footsteps and finds a barefoot boy standing behind him. Without uttering a sound, the boy holds a dirty hand out to him, his round face shining in the blue haze of the distant lights, his nose running with snot that smears across his cheeks.

He finds some quarters in his pocket and gives them to the boy, who grabs them and runs.

He rubs the rosary beads in his pocket, then yanks the rosary from his pocket as he realizes what the star shower in the painting of the robed woman is about. He goes to the window and places his open palms on it. The rosary beads in his left palm scratch the glass in a loud squeak as he stares at the beam of stars, basks in the jealous pleasure of stumbling across this artist. It gorges through his mescal veins, and he wants to keep the identity of the artist unknown to him. There is no sign or signature on the canvas. The star knowledge holds him to the spot as he clutches the black rosary, lifts the beads to the glass, and rubs them into the pane again. The scratch becomes a glassy whine. He swings the rosary above his head, the string of beads whistling faster and faster in a tight circle. The arc of beads crosses the glittering star shield through the glass, dims it momentarily. He recognizes the woman in the blue robes and hurries down the street toward the busy avenida, where the lights of El Paso and Juárez melt into one blinding glow as he approaches the border crossing.

He passes through the pedestrian gates, mutters "American" to the suspicious customs officer, then keeps going, climbs the metal stairs to the narrow walkway spanning the bridge over the Rio Grande. People ahead of him vanish in the glare of the bridge lights. He stuffs the rosary back into his pocket. He reaches the U.S. side, dark and deserted near the parking lots full of cars belonging to people entertaining themselves on the other side. Despite his state, he has no problem finding his pickup truck. He discovers it unlocked, nothing taken from inside. About to climb in, he hears a sound behind him. He turns to find a woman standing behind his truck, a large piece of cardboard clutched in her arms. She yawns, then blinks, then stares at him with swollen black eyes, deep wrinkles in her brown face making him jump quickly into the cab. Her scarf-covered head appears in the rearview mirror. She is blocking his path out of the lot. How did she cross the border and find him? A siren from an El Paso patrol car screams past the lot toward downtown.

He climbs down, dropping the rosary onto the floor of the cab. The woman's cardboard spins through the air and lands in the truck bed. She has disappeared. He runs between cars, searching for her. A moan brings him back to his truck. Approaching, he can see the top of her head in the passenger side of the cab.

He throws open the door to find a rosary on the seat. She is gone. The rosary is not the one the drunk gave him. Its hard beads are bright red and give off a pleasant odor. He inhales the sweet smell of fresh roses. He climbs down to grab the cardboard in the back and throw it away. As he starts to toss it, he notices the penciled markings on its flaps. He carries the cardboard to the light in the cab. Scrawled on the old woman's bed are penciled drawings of mountains and something snakelike, resembling a river. Grease stains cover the rest of the drawing, parts of it smeared with mud. Pieces are torn off. He tosses the cardboard away. It lands in the dirt. He backs out, not remembering to turn on his headlights until he swings onto Stanton Street and a car honks at him. He stops at the traffic light as a crowd of people emerges from the pedestrian bridge. A second cluster follows them. The light turns green. He guns the engine and screeches away.

# THE APPARITION

Carlos waited for the lights to go out in the village, then got up from his bed and went to the window. The cold night had left snow on the peaks of the Sangre de Cristos that made the mountains glow. It was the same light that had made La Virgen de Guadalupe appear to him two weeks ago. He had gone to the bathroom and turned on the light. While taking a piss, he'd glanced at the plastic shower curtain stretched across the tub. The face of La Virgen was illuminated on the curtain. At first, Carlos had thought it was only shimmering drops from the shower that he'd taken earlier that night, but it was a vision—La Virgen de Guadalupe was right there! Her face had not moved under the blue shawl draped over her head, the entire figure appearing in the familiar rainbow colors millions of people worshipped all over the world. As a result of his bathroom discovery, almost five hundred people had trampled through Carlos's house in two weeks. They had seen for themselves, and every single one claimed it was there on Carlos's shower curtain, a true miracle from God. Carlos's bathroom was in the newspapers and on the television news in Albuquerque.

His shower curtain had been famous for fourteen days. Today, the apparition had disappeared. His house was peaceful now. It was the first quiet night after days of letting strangers trample his floors. As he paced in front of the window, he thought of Lucha.

Would the vision of La Virgen make a difference with his old girl-friend? He put on his coat and went out into the winter snap of the New Mexico night. His footsteps crackled in the snow as he turned the first corner. Lucha lived only a couple of streets from his house. As he shivered, he wondered why he had not done this before the apparition. Well, La Virgen had made him brave.

Lucha's house was in the middle of the next block, but he'd rarely seen her since they'd broken up two months ago and agreed to find new lovers. Lucha's mother lived with her and was always interfering. It was hard for Lucha to take care of her and have time for romance. Violeta, Carlos's mother, lived in Belen, south of Albuquerque. Both Carlos and Lucha had lost their fathers in Vietnam, two of seven men from the village who had never come back from the war. It had been several weeks since Carlos and Lucha had run into each other in the *mercado*, but their brief glances then had said enough. No words were spoken, but they knew. During the two weeks of letting people enter his bathroom to share the holiness of the miracle, Carlos had expected Lucha to come see La Virgen. Each day he studied the long lines but never saw her.

Now, as he reached the porch of her house, he hesitated. Above him, the stars seemed to realign themselves. He knocked on Lucha's door. It was almost one o'clock in the morning. After the look she'd given him at the mercado, he was sure she would answer his knock. Lucha opened the door draped in a heavy shawl that covered her nightgown. Her sleepy eyes were hardly open and she didn't seem surprised. Her black hair caught a spray of icy air as she let him in. Carlos entered the warmth of the house, hoping she would be the first to speak, but neither said anything. He wanted to ask her why she hadn't come to see La Virgen. Per-haps she'd saved the newspaper clippings about him, and the apparition was a sign that they could communicate in silence, each sensing what the other was thinking. After all, they had loved each other for three years until the bad days came.

Lucha led him to her bedroom and still wouldn't speak. Carlos was not going to break the silence. He thought of the image on the shower curtain as he followed her.

He was surprised at how quickly Lucha removed her shawl and pulled her nightgown off her shoulders. He took his time removing his coat and layers of shirts. When he got down to his shorts, Lucha lay naked under the blankets. No one had spoken, and he wanted to laugh at their stubbornness. Their determination to stay mute reminded Carlos of the reasons they had stopped being together. As he reached for the sheets, Lucha sat up and slapped him across the face. He staggered back in shock and held his burning cheek.

"What was that for?" he pleaded, tears coming to his eyes.

She pointed to the lump in his shorts. Carlos flung his shorts off. Lucha's whimper was the first sound he managed to get out of her as he slid into her. As they moved together in the black room, Carlos felt like crying. It was a manner of love, this fast sex they'd never shared before. Who had she been seeing? Did Angelo "The Frog" Melendez come to her? As he thrust harder, he recalled seeing The Frog at the mercado on that day he ran into Lucha. As they cried out and came, the image on the shower curtain flashed before him. Afterward, Lucha would not talk to him, and he stared at the ceiling. They fell asleep, Carlos drifting off with sad, cautious contentment.

Two hours later, he awoke to find Lucha snoring. Could he come back to her? Why was she so good at placing him in that vulnerable spot that pounded in his chest each time he thought of her? Carlos rose quietly, put on his clothes, and stepped into the hallway. As he moved slowly through the cold house, he heard a noise behind him. He turned. Carlotta, Lucha's mother, sat in her wheelchair beside Lucha's closed door. He had not seen the old woman in months and was shocked by her appearance. Carlotta's long white hair touched the floor as the thin, broken woman hunched over in her chair like a twisted bug. Her bone-thin hands were permanently gnarled and frozen over her chest. She stared at him with horrifying black eyes, the bones in her face shriveled in the same manner as the fading vision of La Virgen on his shower curtain. Two days before La Virgen totally disappeared, he had noticed how the plastic in the curtain had been cracking in the six-inch area taken up by La Virgen's gentle face.

He wanted to say good morning to Carlotta, but all he could do was stand there as the old woman tried to point a stiff finger toward the door. Her hand trembled in the air, the other one cracking in the stillness of the house as she tucked it under the heavy blankets covering her legs. Carlos moved closer to the front door. The old woman waited. As he reached for the doorknob, he turned to her one last time, but Carlotta was gone. The hallway was empty. No sound of a rolling wheelchair on the wooden floor. He had the urge to wake Lucha, but he opened the front door and rushed out.

The early morning cold bit into his cheeks and made him go faster. He slipped on a sheet of ice as he rounded the corner to his street but caught himself and kept going. When he reached his house, eight people were waiting in front of it. It was six in the morning, about twenty degrees, and there they were. Hadn't they heard that La Virgen was gone? As he stepped onto the porch, some of them bowed and greeted him, a couple of old men making the sign of the cross. Carlos closed the door before any of them could enter. He should have told them to go away, but he couldn't talk right now.

He went into the bathroom and started to take his morning piss.

He saw that a new rainbow had taken shape on the curtain. This time he could not recognize the face hovering on the cold plastic. He wondered if La Virgen was returning for the small audience outside. Carlos flushed the toilet and moved closer to the image, but he could not identify the beautiful face of a woman. It was not La Virgen de Guadalupe. He heard knocking at the door and the restless voices outside. He blinked at the apparition again. This time, he thought it might be Lucha on the curtain. He squinted and moved his eyes inches from the milky blue plastic. No, the woman on his shower curtain was a stranger, her dark brown hair spilling across her shoulders in a style no Virgen would wear, her arms outstretched to the sky. Carlos couldn't tell if she was motioning to him to go away or to come closer. As the knocking on his door grew louder, the image grew brighter. Carlos undressed quickly, carefully parted the curtain, and stepped into the shower. He set the water as hot as he could stand it. When he emerged with a clean, scalded skin, the apparition was still there. He closed the plastic across the tub as drops of water covered the beautiful woman in a warm glow that steamed out of the bathroom and through the house.

## BECKY

Lying here in my bedroom these last few days, I have been thinking about Becky. The snow blowing outside gives my mind time to wander back to the sixth grade and the first girl I ever cared about. I do not stay in bed all day, because the doctor said that would not help me. I remember things better when I move around this big, empty house. I go downstairs into the den and kitchen, make coffee and listen to the radio. I sit in my mother's old rocking chair in front of the fireplace. Looking at the black bricks helps me remember what happened. When I start to feel lonely, I go upstairs and lie down in my room. Under the covers I think about Becky.

In the sixth grade love hit me for the first time. The boys and girls would pair up and say they were going together. I did not have anyone to go with, but my best friend, Doug, was going with Becky, one of the most popular girls in the class. Her short brown hair was perfectly shaped, with bangs hanging down her beautiful forehead, cropped close above her eyes. Doug lived in the opposite direction from where Becky and I did, so he never walked home with us. One day I was walking down the hill from school and spotted Becky several yards ahead of me. We rarely spoke to each other. I was too shy. This time something made me catch up to her. Her hair bobbed up and down as we walked side by side. I had to step faster than usual to keep up with her long strides. She turned and gave me a smile that deepened her dimples. From that day on, we always said "Hi" to each other on the way home. That was it. I lived five blocks from school, and when we reached my house she waved goodbye and continued on.

In the seventh grade, Becky and I were in the same class again, and again we walked home together in silence. We never sat together in class or ate lunch with each other. She continued changing boyfriends every week because it was the thing to do among the popular kids. Of course, I was just the kid who got to walk home with her. I daydreamed about being her boyfriend, but it would never happen, so I never asked her to go with me. In early November, her father, a college professor, got a research job in South America and took his family with him. The last time I saw Becky was at the school Halloween carnival, a few weeks before she left.

On the way home on the day of the carnival, I asked her, "Are you going to the carnival tonight?"

"Yes."

She smiled. "Are you?" She didn't seem to mind that I was talking to her.

"I think so. Will Doug be there?"

"I don't know. He's going with Linda."

"He is?" My heart jumped.

"Sure." She was annoyed. "He and I broke up two weeks ago."

"Can I meet you at the flagpole at seven?" I asked without thinking.

"By the flagpole? Okay."

I giggled nervously and ran into my house.

Inside, I realized that we hadn't told each other what costumes we were going to wear. For the rest of the afternoon I worried about not recognizing her. I agonized over it as I lay in my room, afraid she would not show up at the flagpole because I had not told her what I was going to be disguised as.

MY RECOLLECTION of Halloween is interrupted by the noise outside my window. It has been snowing for three days, and the neighborhood kids are looking forward to the first white Christmas in Albuquerque in many years. Christmas is five days away. I am glad my room is upstairs. I can watch the kids playing in the snow without letting them see me. I don't want them to know I am alone in this house, even though the neighbors were told I would be staying here for several weeks. I hope they don't find out what happened. If they do, I won't be able to be here and think about Becky and Halloween and watch the kids throw snowballs at each other. Flakes fall lightly against the window, and the kids stop the snowball fight to build a snowman. When I was a child, I loved building snowmen during the rare snowfalls. The trouble was my snowmen melted faster than the ones my friends made. Sometimes, my friends would come into my yard and smash my snowmen into disappearing flashes of snow.

I ARRIVED at the flagpole at seven and waited for Becky. Every year the PTA put together games, booths, cakewalks, and a big party. They decorated the classrooms in black and orange crepe paper, with pumpkins, cardboard witches, and the usual Halloween sights. Hundreds of kids and parents came every year, paying fifty cents per person to enter the carnival. The most popular attraction was the haunted house. One of the classrooms had its windows covered with black paper. Volunteers dressed in weird monster costumes and hid inside the cardboard maze walls arranged throughout the room. Candles were placed along the maze to give the blackness an eerie light. It cost ten cents to go through the haunted house.

As I waited for Becky by the flagpole, I decided to ask her to go through the haunted house with me. Couples loved to make out as they giggled through the maze. I made up my mind I was going to kiss her in the darkened room. My Superman costume gave me the courage to do it, though I only wore the top half with my jeans. I had a bright red cape tied around my neck but did not have the courage to wear the blue tights that came with the outfit. I also grabbed an old black Lone Ranger mask from a drawer. I had to wear the mask because it was Halloween, even though Superman didn't wear one.

I waited for half an hour, but no Becky. At seven-thirty the groups of people parking their cars and merrily going inside grew larger. I hurried through the ticket line and squeezed into the crowded lobby. As I grew impatient waiting, costumed kids poured into the school. I waved to the ones I recognized, though several laughed at me and pointed at my costume. I counted several kids dressed in skeleton outfits, the rabbit from Alice in Wonderland, a hobo, two pirates, many cowboys and Indians, and four or five clowns. A couple of girls passed whom I thought were Becky. They had short hair like hers, but their costumes hid their faces. I looked at my watch: it said eight o'clock.

I breathed a sigh of relief when Becky emerged through the crowd of goblins, ballerinas, and fairy princesses. She was dressed as Cinderella in a sky-blue outfit with silver glitter sparkling on the dress. Even though she saw me, she looked to her right as if searching for someone. I reached for her arm and gently pulled her toward me.

"There you are!" She giggled. "You look funny. Superman doesn't wear a mask."

"You are dressed very nice," I managed to say nervously. I felt strange standing with her in front of so many kids who had real boyfriends and girlfriends.

We started down the busy hallway toward one of the game booths, the beanbag toss. We squeezed into the line, and Becky kept turning her head as different boys passed by and noticed her. I wondered if she was self-conscious being seen with me. Both of us spotted Rob at the same time. He was a boy Becky had been going with a couple of weeks before Doug. Rob was an Indian chief, his face streaked with red paint, his head weighed down with a dumb war bonnet of feathers running down his back.

Becky said to me, "Get in line for the haunted house. This beanbag thing is boring. I'll meet you there in a minute."

I hesitated, then left the line as Rob pushed himself against her. Over the sea of masks and hats, Rob and Becky were carrying on an intense conversation that I couldn't hear in the noisy hallway. I found the terribly long line for the haunted house. Black and orange streamers hung from the door, and several were scattered across the floor. Goofy and the Wicked Witch of the West kicked some out of the way as they passed. Shrieks of laughter and hilarious screams echoed from inside the darkened room.

I lost sight of Becky and Rob in the mass of people and stood in line for half an hour before approaching the entrance to the haunted house. A PTA mother, dressed as Caspar the Friendly Ghost, blocked the doorway, taking tickets and trying to control the mob of excited kids and parents. I had been tempted to go find Becky, but she'd said she would join me, and I didn't want to miss her by leaving the slow line. What if she and Rob had gone off together? When my turn came, I searched behind me one last time, then went in.

As I entered the black walls, I was no longer interested in the funny horrors of the haunted house. I wanted to find Becky and be with her. But I followed the cowboy in front of me, and we entered the maze. A witch popped up at the first turn. She was somebody's mother doing her duty for the PTA and didn't frighten anybody. I kept going as kids behind me pushed me in the dark.

My worry over Becky kept me from being startled or frightened by any surprises in the haunted house. I searched for a place in the maze where I could wait for her to come through. I thought of hiding behind one of the black cardboard walls or one of the tall paper skeletons, then found a narrow corner near one of the tables where a lone candle burned. My Superman costume was dark enough to blend into the shadows there. It was a good place to wait.

About ten minutes later, to my delight, Becky came through the maze alone. Rob was not with her. She shrieked as she turned the corner where a witch and a mummy surprised her from behind a sofa. As she approached my corner, I jumped out like Superman does at the beginning of every TV episode. "Boo!" I screamed, louder than the volunteer ghosts and witches had been told to do.

Becky screamed, and her eyes opened wide behind her mask. She gasped for breath. Thirty years later, I do not know if she recognized me in the shadows. In the flickering waves of yellow that the candles threw at the walls, I grabbed Becky in a rough hug and kissed her wetly on the mouth. She gasped, punched me hard on the shoulder, and ran from the haunted house. In her haste, she knocked one of the cardboard walls down. Somebody's mother was caught behind it as she tried to wrestle her wide body into a tight skeleton costume. She saw Cinderella push several kids out of her way, all more shocked by the parent showing her bra and panties than by the fleeing beauty.

I do not remember the rest of that night. It has been a long time since the walls of the haunted house came down on me and blotted out my memory. I don't recall if they threw me out or whether I simply left the carnival and went home alone in the night. Did I finish the maze? Did I hide in its shadows? I do recall that Becky's behavior changed the last few weeks she was there. She started walking home with girls she had never talked to before and never waited for me. I wandered home alone, never certain if this was a sign that she had recognized me in the darkness.

THE SNOW keeps falling. I am angry at my parents. I wish someone were here to keep me company as I think of Becky. Too bad Alvaro left three days ago, having grown tired of picking up the Scrabble letters I kept throwing across the room. If Alvaro was winning the Scrabble game, I would find a reason to throw the board off my bed. I would yell at him to get out of my room. I hope Alvaro has a good Christmas. My parents were paying him well to stay with me. I could tell he didn't like taking care of me. The doctors think someone should be with me at all times, but my parents can't be here with me every day. I don't know why they sent me to this house. I no longer feel any pain, but they were worried about the things I was saying after the accident. If Becky lived in Albuquerque, I would consider marrying her. Certain things have taken place to bring her back into my life, and now I relive Halloween again.

This large house gets very cold. It bothers me to stay in my room without the heat of downstairs. The pajamas and bathrobe don't keep me warm, but since I'm inside all day, I don't feel like getting dressed. It's more comfortable when I want to get in bed and dream about Becky, those dreams coming alive again because it's Christmas and I've received a few gifts already. In the middle of going back to that Halloween, I dreamed about Sarah. Her car is vivid in the dream. Becky shows up in the crowd of pedestrians to help me out of the wreck. She has not aged, and her shiny bangs still bob over her forehead as she finds my broken body. I don't like to think too much about that dream. I'd rather walk through the haunted house with Becky. I can't think about Sarah because my parents say the accident caused all this, why I am stuck in this big house trying to get well. My parents don't realize it is going to be a good Christmas. There are too many good dreams and signs I am in the right house to enjoy the holiday.

My mother called yesterday and told me that next week someone new will be staying with me. She and my father are coming over tonight, and she is cooking dinner. She helped me decorate the Christmas tree downstairs. Dad and I went shopping for my mother's gifts, and I have presents for both of them, plus something special I want to show them. The other day, my mother said it was too bad that none of my friends knew I was out of the hospital. The doctors say it has to be this way for a while. My mother was thinking about my friends because she wished I'd received more get-well and Christmas cards. She felt sad that the big mantel over the fireplace didn't hold a single card. The mantel has always been a favorite place for my parents to display the dozens of cards they get every year. But their cards are in their apartment across town. I have a surprise for them tonight. It arrived yesterday.

The big grandfather clock in the den downstairs chimes at the right time for me, ringing in the morning when I want to go to the kitchen to get something to eat. Today, in this cold bedroom, I waited for the clock but did not hear it. I got up from the bed and put on a sweater under my bathrobe. I passed the window but didn't see any kids playing in the snow, though the whiteness of the empty yard gave me a peaceful feeling. I went down the hall and descended the stairs into the den. The grandfather clock ticked as usual on the other side of the room, and our Christmas tree stood in the corner, covered with tinsel and bright ornaments. In the fireplace across the room, a fire was burning brightly. The room was warm, so the fire must have been burning for several hours.

There was no one else in the house. Who had lit the fire? The flames reflected off the tree ornaments in tiny sparks. I went into the kitchen to make coffee. I put the pot on the stove, then remembered the card. I hadn't looked at it today. I went to the mantel in the den where the lone card stood. I reached over the heat of the fire and held it in my hands. The picture on the front showed a boy and a girl walking across a snowy street toward kids playing in the snow. They were bundled in heavy coats, certainly not for the kind of winters we had in Albuquerque. The boy and girl carried gifts under their arms, and a row of houses dotted the background, while the snow on the roofs was done in white glitter, grainy to the touch. I opened the card carefully. In fancy black letters it said, "Peace On Earth. Good Will Toward Men." At the bottom, in small handwriting, the card was signed in ink: "Merry Christmas. With love, Becky."

When I got the card in the mail yesterday, I wondered, "Who is Becky?" But then I remembered. And the dreams came back.

After thirty years Becky remembered me the way I always wanted.

The doctors said the anxiety attacks will eventually go away. They told me to rest over the holidays.

I carried the card into the kitchen after it arrived and poured myself a cup of coffee. I sat at the table but could barely make out the weather report on the radio because I kept looking at the card. Holding it, I wanted to believe that it really had come from Becky, after all these years, and that no one was playing a joke on me. No one knew about Becky, not even Sarah. I wanted to believe in the memory of walking home with Becky.

Yet, as I stare at the card one more time, I think about Sarah and the funeral. In the silence, I hear the crackling fire, then the sound of an approaching car. I go to the window above the sink and part the curtains to the sight of my parent's station wagon pulling into the icy driveway. It can't be! My mother said they would come tonight, and she always calls first.

I grab the card from the table, turn off the radio, and hurry across the den. About to mount the stairs, I sense a difference in the room. I stop midway up and look down at the cold, empty fireplace. There is no sign of a fire. A chill fills the room as I bound to the top and along the hall. I hear the kitchen door open and run into the bedroom and shut the door. I clutch the card to my chest when I hear my mother calling me from the foot of the stairs. I hear her start to climb and open the card. "Merry Christmas. With love. Becky."

My mother knocks on the door and I close the card. Before she knocks again, I realize the card is from Becky. This time, I know for sure.

# CANYON DE KAYENTA

Frank Martinez and Anne Davis got out of the truck by the side of the narrow dirt road. Two-hundred-foot cliffs towered above them and they saw the rock markers they picked out on their last trip to Canyon de Kayenta.

Anne squinted through her sunglasses and pointed to four narrow pillars that rose at the top. "That's it, isn't it? John said he marked it." She studied the geological map in her hands.

"Yeah." Frank recognized the pillars and climbed into the truck. "Let's go. We're late today."

Anne got in, her face red from the sun and the long trip from Shiprock. The May heat made her curly brown hair stick out from under her cowboy hat. Frank drove in silence. They headed west into a narrow canyon about forty miles southwest of Shiprock, not far from the Arizona border. Frank and Anne were graduate students in archaeology at the University of New Mexico in Albuquerque. They were working on a joint project with students from the University of Texas in El Paso. The couple had been lovers since their undergraduate days, and Anne had been by Frank's side when he suffered a nervous breakdown a year and a half ago. It delayed them beginning graduate school. Now that Frank felt better, they were invited to join the project. In recent months, a previously unexcavated area had been opened by the National Park Service. It was one of the last to be reserved for future archaeologists by scientists who had explored the Four Corners region forty and fifty years ago.

Three weeks ago, Frank and Anne were on the lucky team to uncover the first significant sites found by students. Their group, led by John Fuentes of the Park Service, found a burial site four hundred feet up in a cave behind some cliff houses. In the midst of the white plaster ruins and stone walls, they dug up the mummified remains of an old man who had broken both legs across the shin bones. Frank pointed out in the preliminary report that the fractures had been set so well that only the smallest of bumps were left in the bones. Farther down, in one of the fifty rooms they counted, Anne and two other students found the remains of fourteen infants in a slab-lined cyst used by the Anasazi as a storage bin. Beneath the infants were the bodies of four more children packed in a huge basket. None of the skeletons showed any signs of violence. The team speculated that disease may have swept through the town and killed the children.

Two weeks ago, Frank and Anne, excavating at the infants site, had left the team and gone on a separate dig. They got permission from John to work as a pair for a few days. Anne was her usual curious self over what they found, loved her work, but started to notice that as soon as they left the others, some of Frank's old behavior was coming back. She never would have stepped away from the team without Frank's initiative, but as she noticed his temper grow shorter and his wild determination to be the first at new sites, she began to worry. A deep anger she had not felt since that terrible time a year and a half ago began to build within her as the stark beauty of the desert surrounded their explorations. She noticed he was becoming moodier with each successful find. They had one of their rare arguments about the details of measurements and important facts she wanted to include in their early notes on the old man with the broken legs.

After working alone for two days, they found a burial site near a large kiva. Camping overnight, Frank and Anne worked three full days in uncovering a pair of arms and hands lying side by side on a bed of grass. The elbows touched the wall of the cave in a way that suggested that the rest of the body had not been removed at a later date. Three bracelets of abalone shells were wrapped around the wrists, and two pairs of unworn sandals, patterned in black and red, were lying beside the hands, as was a small basket half full of white shell beads. Another basket nearly two feet in diameter covered the burial. They could not explain the burial and the arrangement of the bones. The rest of the team was brought in and were now in their tenth day of further clearing and cataloging the site. Anne noticed how Frank made sure they were credited in the reports as the discoverers of the site before moving on to their present search for more. It was obvious he was going out of his way to keep the two of them ahead of the others.

Anne loved Frank, but her silent rage for staying with him also kept her going, her determination to be a good student and stay in the field clashing constantly with the way he drove their relationship into the ground. She often wondered if she was unable to admit to herself that she might be using Frank's instability to get herself through school and perhaps see other choices for herself down the road.

Now, as the couple drove down the canyon, Frank thought about their streak of luck. Many archaeologists would spend entire careers trying to find the kind of riches they had found. But they knew this area was abundant with burial sites, places left alone on purpose for years. As students, they were in the right place at the right time, but Frank wanted it to be more than that. If they hadn't made these discoveries, other students would have. His strategy of staying ahead of the others was working, but he didn't know how long John would allow it before letting others explore first.

"Did John mark the distance from Sangre Cliff to the new area?" he asked Anne as the truck, a department vehicle with a UNM logo on the doors, bounced over the rocky ground.

"Yes, half a mile down from the last stake near the central kiva. Is he coming back with Eddie and Laura today?" Cliffs rose higher and closer around them.

"He has to work in Shiprock today. Eddie and Laura are going back for the grant proposal meeting in Albuquerque."

"How come? Are they finished back there? I thought we agreed we'd be at the meeting, too."

Frank shrugged. "What does it matter? They decided to take a break for a couple of days. It was over one hundred degrees yesterday. I gave them our part of the proposal before we left Albuquerque."

"You did? Why didn't you tell me?"

"I forgot."

"Frank! You know we both had to sign it. The Ortiz project was our first grant that got funded. I wanted to see the revised data."

He didn't say a word as he drove slowly over the bumpy ground. Anne removed her sunglasses, rubbed her neck above the collar of her khaki blouse and gave him a distasteful look. Was he finally cutting her out? She stared at the rock walls as they rose even closer on both sides of the truck.

"They must wonder why you and I are out here together," she concluded.

Frank pushed his baseball cap back on his head and felt the sweat run down his back. "I don't care what they think."

"What's wrong with you, Frank?" Anne sat up higher on the

seat. "You're acting like this thing is some kind of race. Why didn't you show me the final grant form?"

As he started to answer, the truck hit a large bump in the road. The tools in the back made a loud crashing noise. He looked at the woman who had been his lover for the last two years and wondered if she realized why this whole thing out here was so important. He slowed down and inched the truck between two huge boulders. It barely cleared the side mirrors, then passed into a wider stretch of canyon.

He hissed at her. "We are out here because you and I know more about the kind of data missing for our book. Plus, we are independent from the rest."

"Independent?"

"That's right." He turned off the engine.

She wanted to slap the hat off his head. "I think you want to be independent from them and from me."

They glared at each other.

"It isn't that way, Anne. I know we've been working hard, but we need to keep going."

They stopped next to a grove of cottonwoods that grew directly below a sheer wall of rock that led up to the rooms they planned to explore. They got out of the truck in silence and gathered their gear and tools. Anne followed Frank as he searched for a way up to the cave. Most of the cliff houses had access by walkways cut into the rock by the Anasazi. This cave was not as high as some they'd encountered. It connected into an area of thirty rooms on the south wall of the canyon.

Frank found the ancient footholds in the rock and heaved himself up. Anne waited for him to ascend several yards before following. He paused every few feet to adjust his backpack and carefully feel the rock as he progressed up the wall. As Anne climbed, she looked across the narrow canyon at the cottonwoods and thick saltcedars that protected a low stone wall surrounding one of the kivas yet to be explored.

The enormous cavern they were approaching arched over the decaying walls. Frank could make out fading petroglyphs on the highest walls, just below the natural arch. This area was rich in valuable finds, and he wondered if such a vulnerable place had been invaded by artifact collectors. He kept climbing and smelled the damp, ancient air as he neared the entrance to the first stone room. He lifted himself over the last ridge above the stairs and stepped through the low doorway. Anne's boots crunched loudly on the stone shard floor as she stopped next to him. They stood in the center of an empty chamber. Silently, they studied the four walls.

"I'm amazed every time at how tightly they fit the stones together," Anne whispered.

She stepped carefully along one wall to a corner, bent low and pulled a notebook from her shirt pocket. She unclipped the pen from her hatband and scribbled a few words.

They paid attention where they stepped, but Frank didn't expect to find much in the front rooms. He could sense when they were near something important but had never shared the feeling with Anne. He entered another room through a low cut in the wall and knelt in the middle of rubble, rocks, and broken adobe slabs. He grabbed a handful of the damp earth and let it fall through his fingers. The chamber had high walls, was dark and enormously quiet. Its roof had caved in, ages ago. He heard Anne scrape something in the other room. As he stared at nothing on the opposite wall, her sounds made him see that their relationship was going to affect the work after all. Why hadn't he taken Eddie's advice and selected a different partner for the entire project. Of course, if he had asked Connie, a fellow student, Anne would have been jealous. As Frank moved through another doorway, he wished they'd made such a working agreement long ago. He wouldn't have needed the Ortiz grant if he had been working alone.

His regrets faded as he passed another twenty yards through a narrow passageway that ended before a second group of rooms. The path was two feet wide and curved back toward the ledge, which dropped two hundred feet to the canyon floor. Anne caught up with him, and they explored the room for three hours without finding anything significant. In the falling gloom and immense silence, they hardly said a word. At one point Anne found what seemed to be a plastic button from a modern shirt. Someone had been here already. Frank searched for carvings and petroglyphs on the walls. In one of the farthest rooms he directed his flashlight at the high walls and spotted something. Anne pointed her flashlight on it, and they saw letters and symbols thirty feet above the floor. They thought it read, "dres cuminya sakoda malo." The letters were painted in dark red.

"That's no ancient language," Frank whispered.

Anne squinted in the beam of the flashlights. "What is it?"

"There seems to be some Spanish in it," he said.

"Conquistadores?"

"No. It looks fairly recent."

"A prank?"

"Maybe," he turned off his flashlight. "But there's no other sign of vandalism or grave theft."

Anne thought she heard something behind them. She swung her flashlight around. Nothing. "Why would someone write that so high on the walls? And how'd they get up there?"

Frank left the room without answering.

They explored several more rooms for another hour, found nothing, and took a lunch break. They went out to the ledge and sat, their feet dangling over the side. Frank drank from his canteen while Anne pulled sandwiches from her bag.

"It's hot," she said and handed him a sandwich, then showed him two pieces of broken pottery. "Look at these."

He examined them. "Small pieces, but you may have found what we've been looking for."

She waited for further clues to what he meant. She looked at his brown face, clean shaven as always, now glistening with sweat, and his long hair tied back in a ponytail. She poured water on her bandanna and wiped the sweat from her face.

Frank gazed across the canyon as waves of heat shimmered in the blinding sunlight. Distant mountain ranges waved on the horizon as if they were moving toward him. "We'll start again in a minute."

"A minute? We just sat down to eat. My feet hurt."

"Show me where you found these and I'll start."

"Frank! What's the hurry? We've been working our asses off. Why do you have to push it every day? We might miss something."

He glared at her and threw the shards of pottery back at her. They bounced off her chest and one of them flew over the ledge.

Anne was stunned. "What the hell was that for?"

"I'm tired of this, Anne," Frank started. "You know how important this is, but you don't seem to want to do as much as we said we would."

"You asshole." She rose to her feet, dizzy from the height. She moved into the shadows until she couldn't see the canyon floor.

Frank got up. "You and I have done some great projects, but we agreed we can't act precious around each other. We have to work as a team."

"What?" She raised her voice, and it boomed across the cave. "You bastard! All you care about is digging holes and getting credit for everybody's hard work!"

He felt like hitting her, though the rush of violence surprised him as it came and went. He placed his hands on his hips. "You know how we talked about having the chance to go to Mexico with that National Geographic team next year?"

"So?" She didn't want to talk anymore.

"Well," he hissed. "I see now it would be a mistake to go together. I want to apply with the Park Service as soon as possible. John says I have a good chance. I want to get out of Albuquerque. He says the job in Tucson pays good money and I can have my own projects."

"You never told me this," she snapped. "Do what you want. I don't care. I'm going to Albuquerque tonight."

"Tonight? You can't do that." He folded his arms over his chest.

"Yes, I can." She moved farther away from him. "If you won't take me back, I'll call John to come get me." She picked up her backpack.

"We can't go back until tomorrow and you know it." He hoped she didn't hear the panic in his voice. "We have work to do here."

"You selfish bastard. Work is always it. How much time have we had together in the past year?"

"What does that have to do with anything?"

Anne took off her hat and wiped the sweat. "Nothing, Frank. It has to do with nothing because it's not part of this work." She sighed. "Let's get to work. I need more notes. I'll complete my part of the report, but I'm going back tonight." She hurried into the next room to explore.

Frank followed her without a word. He was furious and fought to keep his mouth shut but was relieved it was all finally out. Anger pounded in his heart.

They entered a rectangular room that was very dark and smelled different than the other chambers. Anne stepped gingerly to the west wall and knelt near the middle of it. She pointed to a high place in the rocks twenty feet above them. There were two animals resembling deer painted in blue beside a red sun symbol. The ancient drawings were perfectly preserved. At earlier sites, Frank noted that if there were well-preserved drawings in a room, it usually led to some kind of discovery.

He knelt beside Anne and hoped she had calmed down.

"Turn and face the north wall," she told him.

"Why?" He did as she said.

"Look down low off the floor. Do you see the rise in it? Over there."

Frank crouched, pointed his flashlight, and bent his head six inches off the floor. He studied the wall from that view. "Some kind of mound down there," he said excitedly.

"Yeah. Should I mark it?"

"Wait. Let's measure the area and dig a little."

They moved forward on their knees and stopped ten feet from the north wall. Frank reached out to the mound with both open hands and carefully shifted his weight forward. Suddenly, his right arm sank through the earth.

"Watch out!" Anne startled them both with the loud echo of her voice.

"It's okay. Not deep. Just a couple of feet." Frank sat back, wiped the dirt from his arms and removed picks and brushes from his pack. "Oh, hell!"

"What?" Anne asked as she emptied her pack.

"I left both shovels in the truck."

"I'll go get them."

She surprised him with the offer. Frank twisted around on his knees to find her in the beam of the flashlight. "You'll be okay climbing down and up?"

"Who do you think I am?" she sneered, the anger returning. She left the room quickly as he started clearing a small area with his hands, a highly inappropriate procedure for such a delicate site.

The dirt around the hole sank as the opening grew, and the grave opened before him. His heart beat faster as he reached for the flashlight. There was something inside. He aimed the beam and bent low. He could make out a mummified figure covered by objects he couldn't see yet. He began enlarging the hole with a small pick. The damp earth and layers of stones and pebbles fell into the black air below. A dank, musty smell rose into the room. Frank had never smelled it so strongly before and coughed in the rising dust. He loved the detailed, intricate work of scraping and brushing, inch by inch. It took discipline to settle into excavating things from the past, sacred objects, bones, and past lives taken from their ancient resting places into scientific history. It was the taking that he loved.

After twenty minutes of careful digging, he measured the space already exposed, with special string previously cut into specific units, then continued digging with the pick. He realized he didn't need the shovels Anne had gone for. The dirt around the grave was loose. He finished opening the top layer as he heard Anne's footsteps behind him. As he waited for her to enter the room, he saw that the large grave had clearly been set against this wall for a purpose. The outline of a curved masonry wall was slowly starting to appear through the falling door and emerging floor. Inside the grave was the tightly flexed body of an old man lying on his left side. His hair was streaked gray and tied back in a bob. A billet of wood served as a pillow. The body's outer wrapping was a feather blanket. Beneath the feather cloth was a white cotton blanket, excellently made and appearing as clean and new as if freshly woven. Beneath the white covering was an old gray cotton blanket. Beneath that one, lying on the mummy's breast, was a single ear of corn. A red mat covered the floor of the grave. The amount and variety of objects laid away with the body suggested that the individual had been highly respected in life. A wooden digging stick, broken to fit the grave, lay across the burial bundle. Besides this, and also broken, was a bow so thick that only a powerful arm could have pulled it. With the bow was a single reed arrow with a fire-hardened wooden point. Five pottery jars, one broken, together with four bowl-shaped baskets woven from yucca leaves, were also in the grave. These were filled with cornmeal, shelled corn, four ears of husked corn, pinion nuts, beans, and salt. He ran his flashlight over and over this scene, already composing detailed descriptions of everything in his racing mind.

Frank was too hypnotized to notice that Anne had not entered after he had heard her footsteps. Finally, he snapped out of his reverie. He'd been looking at what could be one of the most important archaeological finds in the state in years. He rose and rubbed his sore knees. He faced the doorway of the room, but there was no sign of Anne. He left the room carefully and searched the hallways near the site. "Shit," he muttered and went outside.

He peered over the ledge to the truck at the bottom. Anne should have been back by now. What were those footsteps he'd heard behind him? He went to the stone steps, but there was no sign of her. Could she have fallen?

"Anne!" he shouted in a booming voice that reverberated across the canyon.

It faded and silence returned. He thought he heard a noise from the room where he'd made the incredible discovery and hurried to it. But she wasn't in there. He knelt down in front of the grave and stared at his treasure. The temptation to reach down and touch the feathers was very strong. He would be doing everything the wrong way if he started touching the beautiful array of objects.

He sat on the dirt floor and stared at his discovery. Eddie would never believe it. This had to be the most impressive find any student team had ever made. He had done it again, but they would say he and Anne had done it. He rose and went to look for her again. She had been gone for more than half an hour.

"Anne! Anne! Where are you?" A million voices jumped across the great arch hundreds of feet above him.

As his voice died away, he thought he saw something move between rooms along the walkway to his left. He waited, then started to panic. He went from room to room for another fifteen minutes and came out onto the sunlit walkway, the sound of falling rock startling him.

Anne stood there silently, her cowboy hat gone, her head bathed in sweat. Her hair clung to her head in wet knots, and her blouse was soaked. One cheek was streaked with the fine white dust that filled some of the rooms. He had never seen her like this.

"Where were you?" he asked nervously, trying not to scream at her.

"I got lost," she barely whispered.

"Lost? How could you get lost? That room isn't hard to find."

"I didn't go to the truck." Anne moved closer to him. A necklace hung around her neck. She tucked it inside her blouse.

"Where did you go?" he asked. "And, where did you get that?" He pointed to her wet neck.

Anne raised a hand slowly and rubbed the green and yellow beads. "I went to explore by myself." She smiled for the first time and sat on a large rock. "I figured you could do your work without me."

"What's with you?" Frank raised his voice. "Quit acting so weird. I can't believe you'd actually take off by yourself, make me worry. Plus, you know damn well not to take anything, much less wear it around your neck!" He started to leave, intent on returning to his discovery. "Put it back where you found it and I won't report this."

Anne rose and tottered dangerously close to the ledge. "I want to go back to Albuquerque tonight," she said. She closed her eyes.

"Do you think I am going to do that and leave this fantastic thing? Huh? Do you really fucking think I am going to do that?"

"That fantastic thing is gone," she said without expression.

"What?" He ran through the empty, brown corridors of earth.

Anne slowly followed. When she made her way into the room, he was on his knees, flashlight on, leaning over the deep chasm.

"What happened?" he gasped. "Dammit! Tell me what happened, Anne!" He stumbled to his feet. They heard rock falling below them.

"I came in here when I heard you calling me," she said, her voice calm. "You weren't here. As I started to leave, I turned on my flashlight and saw that the whole thing had caved in. I think it fell several levels down."

Frank leaped at her and grabbed her roughly by the arms. "See what you did," he hissed in her ear. "If everything had been done the right way, this wouldn't have happened. You should have just gone and got the shovels!"

"You didn't need them." She pushed him away. "If you'd kept digging, the whole thing would have collapsed anyway. You opened it too quickly, Frank! You did it the wrong way, and you know it! I didn't do this. You did. You could have waited for me and the rest of the team to help open everything up, but you couldn't wait. You caused the cave-in."

Frank slapped her. They both froze in the shock of it.

She ripped the necklace off her neck and threw it at him.

Frank caught it in midair as she rushed out. He let her go. He wanted to see how badly damaged the grave was. The flashlight revealed a fine layer of dust hanging in the air. He peered over the fragile edge as more rubble fell in. He could barely make out the broken body of the mummy, which had landed about ten feet below its original resting place. Layers of rock, brick, and dirt covered the blankets. The delicate pottery jars were smashed. He could not see the huge bow and red mat. It would take days of climbing down into dangerous and collapsing floors to recover every piece. He would need special permission for a risky descent and figured the Park Service would not grant it once they found out about the sloppy work. Would Anne tell John the whole story? He wished he had a tarp to cover the hole and protect his find, regardless of the shape it was in. He would go back to the team's base camp, get a tarp, take Anne back, and not tell anyone about what had happened. He would return tonight.

As he left the room, he heard the truck start. He ran to the ledge in time to see Anne drive away. He scampered down the narrow steps, slipped a few times but caught himself. By the time he reached the canyon floor, she was long gone. His sleeping bag and camping gear lay on the ground. A note was propped against the bag: "You can go back with John tomorrow. I will tell him where you are. He'll come out tonight." She hadn't signed it.

Tears of anger and frustration ran down his cheeks, and he tore his cap from his head. As he gathered his gear to move under the cottonwoods, he looked toward the cave. He imagined the old man standing up there, the huge bow cocked and with an arrow aimed straight down at him. He shook his head.

Now that Anne had left, a silence and sense of being alone filled him and passed through the ancient air of the canyon. He slumped down on the sleeping bag, exhausted. He took out his notebook and tried to recapture the details of his discovery. But he could jot down only a few words—"Canyon de Kayenta. Old man. Corn. Great man died alone." Then he stopped, closed the notebook, and fell into an exhausted sleep.

Frank was startled by falling rocks. The early evening sunset flushed the top walls of the canyon in a blinding red light that faded to a blue darkness below, where the sun could not penetrate. He looked up. A face appeared in the entrance to the cave, then vanished the instant Frank pointed his flashlight there. For the first time in all of his years of exploring the desert, he was scared. He stepped out from under the trees and raised the flashlight again. There was nothing up there. He managed a short laugh and wondered when John would arrive. As the supervisor, he would ask Anne what had happened, and she would tell him. He thought about their quarrel, and a wave of anxiety filled his heart. He picked up his pack, grabbed one of the shovels that had started the whole incident, and headed toward the steps. He climbed several feet to a shelf of rock where he could see anyone coming up the canyon, then sat and waited for John. A couple of times he heard falling rock but did not look up. He leaned against the wall for another nap.

An hour later, he opened his eyes in the pitch blackness of the canyon. He heard the approaching truck, saw the beam of the headlights. The oncoming vehicle maneuvered carefully through the boulders, the headlights throwing strange patterns against the shadows of the canyon. John stopped the truck in front of the cottonwoods, beside Frank's gear, and left the headlights on as he stepped from the truck.

"Frank! Frank! It's John! Where are you?"

John had rescued lost students before, but he'd been surprised by what Anne had told him about Frank. He heard rock falling and saw the cave. A wild flashlight beam bounced from wall to wall at the top. It might have been a signal, but it disappeared after a few seconds.

"Frank!" He called again.

The beam reappeared. He pulled his flashlight from the truck and headed toward the steps. What was Frank doing up there? It was dangerous to work at night. As he started his ascent, John heard a crash and ducked. Several rocks rolled by.

"Frank!" he cried and climbed faster.

He aimed his flashlight in the darkness of the narrow steps and caught Frank at the top, twenty feet above him. John was angry and had plenty to say to Frank, but those thoughts vanished when he saw the expression on Frank's face. Frank did not move as John reached the top. Out of breath, John froze as his flashlight found the beautiful feather blanket and red mat Frank held in his arms. Then he saw the white dust and blood caked on the student's face, a mask of ancient dirt streaking darkly as tears of triumph ran down Frank's cheeks.

# INVISIBLE COUNTRY

Mario rose from his crouching position behind the pile of tumbleweeds to get a better view of the two Border Patrol officers pulling the body from the Rio Grande. He knelt down again when he thought one of them spotted him across the swollen river. They struggled up the bank, the heavy, bloated body between them. When they disappeared in the tall cattails, he let out his breath. He didn't think they would return to the water's edge. He had seen the drowned man trying to cross the river an hour before the Border Patrol van had pulled into the cottonwoods beside his grocery store, whose back faced the water, which was twenty feet from his fence. Mario saw many things from there—high school kids partying naked, and trucks from the cement plant dumping strange-colored chemicals in the water. Most of all, Mario observed the people who hurried through the thick vegetation across the river. The majority were illegal aliens from Mexico. Mario had gathered tumbleweeds, tree trunks, pieces of wood, and the rusting frame of a 1953 pickup truck against the fence, a mass of junk and wild growth like any other spot along the river. It was the ideal place to hide and watch whatever came by.

He liked to get out of the store each day after the evening rush. As the owner of the only grocery store in town, he talked to many people every day. Dealing with so many people made him nervous. Therefore, each evening he left Neto, the boy he hired to help him, in charge, unlocked the back gate to his property, closed it behind him, and found a comfortable spot in the camouflaged area. There, he sat on one of the logs and gazed across the rapidly flowing water. Most nights, there was nothing to see. Across the river, rolling hills led west into the desert. Sometimes, things happened to change the deceptively peaceful atmosphere. Each day, Border Patrol vehicles drove along the opposite bank but rarely stopped. A Border Patrol van was the last thing he usually saw before returning to his store. A half hour of gazing was all he needed. Then he was calm enough to help Neto clean up for the nine p.m. closing. He rarely missed his nightly escape to the river.

That evening, he had not seen the man drown, but witnessing the Border Patrol agents pulling him out was the most disturbing thing he'd seen in all of his years of watching the river. Where did they take dead illegal aliens? He was about to return to his store when he saw one of the officers through a gap in the cattails on the opposite bank. The man drew his gun from his holster and looked down at the ground. The gunshot echoed across the water. A cloud of blue smoke rose around the officer, who holstered his gun and disappeared.

Mario had seen them dump the body into the back of the van, so what was the officer shooting at? He rose ten minutes later and went to help Neto close. Rounding the corner of the building, he heard car motors in the distance.

SEVERAL DAYS PASSED. Mario thought about the incident constantly. He was fifty-four years old, and things like this troubled him deeply. He had a hard time sleeping. He wanted to tell someone what he had seen. Who or what had the officer shot? He searched the newspaper for a story about a drowning but found nothing. Several days after it happened, he almost called Roberto, the local sheriff, but replaced the receiver on the telephone without dialing. He had known Roberto for a long time, but something kept Mario from calling him. He knew that Border Patrol agents did wrong things from time to time. Friends of his had been harassed, questioned by aggressive officers about their nationality. Some had been accused of being wetbacks. A few had been falsely arrested as illegals, then released without apology when they proved they were U.S. citizens. These things happened along the border all the time.

One week after the incident, a Border Patrol agent walked into Mario's store. It was early in the afternoon. The place was empty. Neto was cleaning the small freezers in the back of the store. Mario was doing the bookkeeping in the ledgers he kept behind the counter that served as his desk.

The officer strolled slowly toward him. He looked at Mario, his eyes hidden behind sunglasses.

"Do you work here?" the officer asked him in a quiet, even tone.

"I am the owner of this store," Mario answered. He closed the ledger and set it aside.

"How long have you been in business?" the officer asked. His hidden eyes roamed the shelves of canned goods, bread, and soda cans.

"I have been here twenty-five years," Mario answered. He felt his chest tightening, but he was surprising himself with his ability to talk to this man.

"That's a long time," the officer said as he turned back to look at him directly. He removed his sunglasses and set them gently on the glass counter. "You must see many things going on in this town."

"What do you mean?" Mario asked. The doorbell rang, and Leo, one of the many unemployed men in town and one of Mario's closest friends, strolled in. Leo came in to chat around this time every afternoon. Mario gave him credit against his unemployment checks and sometimes a free Coke or coffee.

The officer placed both hands level on the counter and leaned forward. Mario shifted his feet and moved a rack of beef jerky closer to the counter. He had not broken out in a sweat as he thought he would.

"You know lots of things that happen in this area," the officer went on. "That's what people tell me around here."

Leo took a newspaper off the stack by the door. Mario could tell that he was listening closely.

"Like what?" Mario asked the officer. His anger was starting to emerge. He was surprised the conversation was going this well.

The officer sighed and pulled a bag of beef jerky off the rack. He spoke as he tried to open the stiff plastic. "I'm investigating a murder that took place near here a few days ago. I know a lot of wet—Excuse me. I know many illegal Mexicans cross near here, and I'm wondering if you've seen anything unusual lately." He stared at Mario with clear green eyes.

Mario wasn't nervous. "We've had vandalism around here, but that's been going on for years. I see people cross the river sometimes, but they just pass through on their way to somewhere else." Leo shuffled the pages of his newspaper. Mario wondered where Neto was.

"The people we suspect of this murder may not be illegals." The officer took his first bite from the string of meat, made a face, then chewed slowly.

"Have you talked with the sheriff?" Mario asked. He was breathing a little harder and wanted to be friendly to this man. He knew he was not one of the agents who had pulled the body out of the water.

The officer seemed annoyed by Mario's question. He stepped back from the counter. "I wanted to check with some of the people around here first. Have you ever seen people with drugs across the river? Be easy for somebody like that to cross behind your store."

"No." Mario swallowed.

As if on signal, Leo walked to the counter. "Hello, Mario. Just the paper today." He did not look at the officer.

"Hello, Leo." Mario breathed. "I'm sorry, officer. I can't help you." He rang up the quarter for the paper.

The officer looked at Neto as the boy appeared from the back room. "Thanks anyway," he said and quickly walked out without paying for the jerky.

Mario let him go.

The green patrol car churned up a cloud of dust as it left the dirt lot.

"What was that all about?" Leo asked.

"I don't know," Mario said. He couldn't tell Leo about what he had witnessed.

"I've never seen *la Migra* in here before," Neto said in his squeaky voice. "Man, something must be happening for them to come around here."

"Yeah," muttered Mario as he pulled out the ledgers. Leo was watching him closely.

That evening, Mario took his usual break, leaving Neto in the store and strolling around the building, feeling self-conscious as he made his way through the junkyard. He looked around several times, half-expecting the officer who had visited him to pop from behind a tree. He stepped over an old car tire, then sat in a crooked folding chair he'd placed behind the stack of wood after the incident with the agents. He wanted to be able to watch for a long time.

As the evening grew darker, there was nothing to see except the familiar change of color in the sky. The clouds in the west brushed into layers of red as the sun went down. The river ran straight and fast, the late sky shimmering on the water in long ribbons of gray light. Sometimes, the dance of evening colors brought Mario a memory of his recurring dream of a desperate attempt to cross the river. In the dreams, Mario rose from the muddy water. His head and clothes dripped with slime and mud. His arms flailed in the air. He couldn't see anything for a few smothering moments. His cries for air went unnoticed. No one was there to help him out of the water, to keep him from drowning. As he gasped and crawled up the bank, his clothes transformed themselves into a clean white. By the time he had stumbled back to his store, he was no longer covered in mud. He leaned against his front door, absolutely dry, fumbled for his keys, then unlocked the door to find his long dead father and mother, covered in the same river mud, cleaning the store. The sight of his parents woke him up.

Sometimes Mario would gasp awake, caught in the rush of the dream. Other times, he would awaken in a peaceful daze despite the dream's last few moments. Sometimes he thought about the dream when he came to his hiding place. He had no idea what it meant because he had never fallen or gone swimming in the river. He was born in El Paso, was not an illegal from Mexico who'd attempted to cross. The dreams had started three years ago. There had been no dreams since the drowning he'd witnessed.

Now, as it grew darker, Mario thought that if it weren't for business, he would come here earlier in the day to see what went on in broad daylight. He looked across the river, anticipating the first patrol vehicle. Why had the officer questioned him? Had the others spotted him and sent today's agent to check him out? The sound of an approaching car broke into his thoughts. He could tell the direction and distance of motors after hearing so many patrol cars go by. Mario looked to his right and saw an old pickup on the opposite bank. He had never seen this one before. It moved slowly through the trees.

The pickup stopped fifty yards upriver. Mario couldn't see what the two men in the truck looked like. He recalled the agent's question about drugs. He got up from the chair and moved closer to the fence. He pushed a couple of logs aside to get a better look. One man climbed out of the passenger side and went to the back of the truck. He leaned into the bed and shuffled boxes around. Mario looked at his watch. The man climbed back into the truck. It started moving. It was directly across from Mario when it stopped again. The truck idled for a few moments. Then the driver turned on his headlights. The truck went another hundred yards along the bank before turning onto the levee road that led into town. Mario sighed. As he grew curious about a truck he had never seen before, he told himself to do something about what he had seen, days ago. Who would listen to him? Most complaints against Border Patrol agents were never investigated by the authorities. Could he tell a convincing story?

He walked back to the store to find that Neto had finished cleaning and was waiting for him to lock up so he could go home. Neto never asked where Mario went on his breaks. Mario assumed the boy knew he was always in the back.

"I was worried," Neto said as he stepped inside. "I didn't know where you were."

"Just out back," Mario answered. "Sorry I took so long."

He went to the cash register to close it out. Neto stood across the counter with a worried look on his face.

"Was it that Migra guy? Did he come around again?"

Mario shook his head. Since the officer's visit, the boy had been quieter than usual. In a way, it made Mario feel good that someone was worried about him. He knew Leo was also watching him closely.

Neto shrugged. "When I went to lunch after he left, I saw two Migra cars parked at Roberto's office."

Mario counted the bills in the register. "Why don't you go home, Neto. I'll close up. Everything looks fine for tomorrow. Take off."

"Are you sure?" Neto had never hesitated about leaving before.

"Go on. I'll see you tomorrow."

He watched the boy go. The dim ceiling lights cast a blue glow over the neat rows of cans and boxes. Mario finished in half an hour, checked the windows and back door, then stepped out the front door and locked up.

He was unlocking the door of his old yellow Mustang when headlights came on across the street. The patrol van came out of the night and pulled in behind his car. Mario placed his keys in his shirt pocket as the van lights went off. Two officers stepped out.

"Hold it right there," one of them said in a loud voice.

They were the two officers who'd pulled the body out of the river.

The second one held a clipboard casually at his side. The first man rested his right hand on his holstered gun.

Mario stifled a deep urge to run. "What's the problem?"

The two men stood on either side of him. "We've had reports that you've been hiding wetbacks in your store," the one with the clipboard told him.

Mario smelled the sweat and the lotion on the men. One of them sported a crewcut and was very tall. The agent with the clipboard was older, with graying hair. He acted like he was in charge.

"I don't know what you mean," Mario answered, his heart pounding. "I would never do anything like that."

"We know who you are," the officer continued. "You've had

this place for a long time, but it looks like all of a sudden you've decided to be a local hero for these wetbacks. We could arrest you right now." His partner glared at Mario. He was the one who'd fired the gun. No one moved.

Mario felt dizzy. "Why are you doing this?" he managed to ask, even though he had the answer. "Another officer came to talk to me."

He leaned against his car to try to get rid of his dizziness. He breathed evenly as he waited for something to happen. The silence was broken by the van's squawking radio. The tall man went to answer the call. Mario couldn't make out the quick radio exchange, but it made both men climb back into the van. Thinking they were going to leave, he breathed a sigh of relief. But they sat in the van for several more excruciating minutes, blocking his car. He was afraid to get into the car or make a wrong move. The cool night chilled the sweat that ran down his back. Would they shoot him to get rid of their witness? There was no one else around.

The van's engine started with a roar that startled Mario. He was suddenly afraid that they would ram his car as a warning. But the van backed up slowly and pulled out of the lot, picked up speed and turned down a street that led to the nearest bridge. Mario brushed his slick black hair back from his sweating forehead and climbed into his car.

That night, he hardly slept. At five in the morning he rose and ate breakfast. He usually got to the store by seven for the nine a.m. opening. This day, he dressed early and left his house in the morning darkness. A mid-September fog hung over the valley. It floated over the river in long stretches of heavy whiteness. Mario drove past his store and turned down the street toward the bridge. Scattered houselights from early risers cut through the fog that hung between the small houses. The high street lamps and the lights on the railroad crossing burned in the mist, their globes illuminating the coming dawn. He looked both ways and drove carefully over the tracks. The final minutes of night blanketed everything. It looked like the fog had taken the whole town away, leaving only the white gleam of the river.

He crossed the bridge to the west side of the river, turned right on the levee road, and followed the narrow dirt strip along the water. The cottonwood trees and rows of mesquite bushes protruded through the mist, Mario's low headlights illuminating their thick black branches. Twisted shapes hung over the road, limbs scratching against Mario's car as he weaved through them. He stopped directly across from his store. The fog was too thick to see clearly to the other side, but he knew where he was. He turned off the engine and the headlights, surprised at how brightly the fog floated in the night air. As he got out, he heard a barking dog across the river—Rudy's dog, down the street from his store.

He walked carefully toward the bank, pushing green limbs aside, stumbling a couple of times in the wet reeds and sticky cattails, unafraid as he heard the low sound of the rushing water. He stood near the spot where the officer had fired his gun. Somehow, in the eerie morning darkness, he felt that this was the exact spot. Without a flashlight, he couldn't see anything on the ground. Anyway, he didn't know what he was looking for.

Rudy's dog barked again at the same instant the vehicles broke the eerie calmness of the river. Two sets of headlights moved slowly through the fog. They came from opposite directions, a hundred yards apart and heading for Mario's car. He crawled several yards away and crouched under a mesquite bush. He heard the idling engines, then car doors slamming. He got down on all fours and felt the cold, wet mud penetrate his clothes. He heard men crashing through the trees. Twigs snapped as they pushed through the mass of mesquite. When they reached the river, the footsteps stopped. Mario trembled in the dampness and chill. It would be daylight soon. The fog would not hide him much longer.

He heard three different voices. He got down flat on his belly as they drew nearer. He scratched his face in the dark but managed to roll farther under the mesquite. The men trampled around him, not speaking. He couldn't tell if they were agents. He was afraid they would use flashlights. As he waited, water oozed through his pant legs, its cold movement pressing him harder into the ground. He closed his eyes. The men moved away from him. Car doors closed. The vehicles drove away.

Mario's back hurt as he crawled out. The early morning light clarified the vegetation around him. His car sat undisturbed. Whoever they were, the men could identify his yellow Mustang. If they were waiting out there in the fog, they could get him when he drove off. He couldn't stay there any longer. He did not turn on his lights as he drove quickly toward the bridge. The fog started to lift as the first aura of sunrise formed to the east. As he entered his store's dirt lot, he saw Roberto and Leo standing by the sheriff's car.

"Good morning, Mario," Roberto said, a worried look on his face as Mario climbed from his car. "How are you?" His eyes went to Mario's mud-stained pants and shirt.

"Hey, Roberto, Leo. What's going on so early?"

"We need to talk," Roberto told him and patted him on the back.

Mario avoided looking at either of the men as they entered the cold building. Roberto motioned to them to sit at the tiny folding table Mario kept near the front for coffee drinkers. Mario finally looked at Roberto. He should have told him everything that first day.

"A Border Patrol officer came by to tell me about an investigation they are doing. I don't know if you heard about the drug bust across the river a couple of weeks ago. One of the men they arrested was Lalo Acosta. I don't know if you knew him. He'd lived in town for about six months."

Roberto paused as Leo motioned that he was going to make coffee in the brewer Mario kept on the counter. "Anyway," Roberto continued, "they found Acosta murdered across the river from here. I'm not sure why the Border Patrol is involved. They usually leave this kind of stuff to us and the FBI in El Paso. I thought it was just another drug thing until Leo came by early this morning to tell me a Border Patrol officer came in here to ask you questions. Mario, what does this Acosta thing have to do with you?" Roberto shifted in his seat and set his cowboy hat on the table.

He brushed the mud and grass from his knees. "I don't know this Acosta, but I think they killed him."

"What?"

"I think the Border Patrol shot someone across the river, over a week ago. I was out behind the store taking a break and saw two of them pull a body out of the water. Then, a few minutes later one of them fired his gun at something on the ground. I don't know what it was because I think they'd already dumped the body in their van."

Mario blurted it out so fast that the two other men just stared at him. Leo placed his arm on Mario's shoulder. Mario hung his head and wept quietly. "I didn't think they saw me watching them, but the same two agents threatened me yesterday." He told them about the encounter beside his car.

Roberto scratched his chin and frowned. Leo had not said a word.

"Why didn't you come talk to me?" Roberto asked.

"I couldn't."

"Why not?" Roberto raised his voice impatiently.

"I don't know.

"Why were you hiding back there, Mario?" Leo asked. They were the first words he'd spoken.

Mario shrugged. "Not really hiding. I go behind the store to look at the river. I just happened to be out there when it happened."

Roberto stared out the windows. "The officer who spoke to me said they found Acosta shot in the head. He didn't say anything about a drowning. Why would two Border Patrol agents shoot a drug suspect, and if he was already dead when they pulled him out, why would they shoot him?"

Leo brought cups of coffee to Mario and Roberto.

Roberto rose without touching his coffee. He put his hat on and started to leave. "I'm going to have Teddy and Juan patrol around here more often. If anything comes up, call me right away. I just wish you had told me sooner, Mario." He didn't wait for a response but closed the door quietly behind him.

Neto would be in soon, thought Mario, to get things going for the day.

"What are we going to do, Mario?" Leo asked in a low voice.

"I don't think you have to worry, Leo." Mario sighed. "Perhaps, all this is nothing. I don't really know what I saw."

Nothing happened for the next four days. Mario was grateful for Roberto's deputies patrolling by the store. He didn't go behind the store during those days. He saw no green vans during those four days.

The following Saturday brought heavy rains to the valley, and the river rose. By Sunday morning part of the town was flooded. Hardly anyone came into Mario's store. Neto didn't work on Sunday, so Mario spent the day mostly alone. The parking lot was a lake. Mario spotted an occasional sheriff's car on the street. A couple of hours before closing time, Leo came in and invited

Mario to eat dinner with him at Sylvia's Cafe. He'd just cashed his unemployment check. Mario said he didn't feel like it. Leo said he'd come back at closing time to see if Mario had changed his mind.

Mario found his plastic raincoat in the storeroom and an old pair of boots he hadn't worn in years. He pulled them on and went out into the rain. The water in the lot hadn't quite reached porch level, but another day of heavy rain would threaten the store. He pulled the coat's yellow hood over his head and splashed through the mud to the back. He opened the gate to find that the rain had washed much of the junk away. Tree trunks and wood hung over the bank above the roaring water. As he kicked soaked weeds and pieces of cardboard aside, part of his wooden fence fell into the river.

He reached to save some of the fence and slipped and almost fell into the river. He scooted back on his rear, pushing himself with his hands. More of the fence dropped into the water. Mario rolled onto his knees and stood up. He wiped the rainwater off his face as the two agents entered the gate. The men's faces were hooded in olive green raincoats. Mario stared through the pellets of rain. The men kept their hands hidden under the plastic. As Mario moved away from the bank, one of them showed him the revolver under the coat. Mario tried to move to his left, slipped in the mud, and dove into the remaining pile of tree trunks and car tires. As he rolled, one green raincoat surged toward the disintegrating edge of the bank.

Mario's eyes stung with water as someone pushed the agent into the river. Flat on his stomach, Mario tried to reach for a long stick wedged under a tire. The first gunshot tore above his head. He pushed his body deeper into the logs. They fell on top of him. He watched Leo wrestle with the second agent. The logs were crushing him. He pushed against them, and the ground beneath him gave way. As he tumbled amid the logs rolling toward the river, his hand shot out and clutched the broken fence. Leo and one of the agents fell past him into the river and were swept away. Mario heard sirens. He hung on, inches from the roaring water. Roberto and four deputies appeared, guns drawn. Hands reached for him, pulled.

WHEN HE AWOKE in the Las Cruces hospital the next morning, Roberto was standing by his bed, the bright sunlight of a clear day sparkling off the shiny badge on his chest. Mario tried to turn his head, but the tubes in his nostrils wouldn't let him.

"Leo?" he managed.

Roberto pinched his hat in his fists. "I'm sorry, Mario. Leo drowned."

Mario's tears blended into patterns of light he was used to seeing in his dreams of the river. "And the two agents?"

"One drowned. The other has been arrested. The FBI thinks Acosta was a drug runner for a group of agents."

"Leo was coming to take me to eat at Sylvia's."

"I know," said Roberto. "He called me yesterday when he saw one of the green vans waiting across from Sylvia's. I wish he'd waited for us. When you feel better, I have to get a statement from you."

"Leo saved my life."

Roberto nodded. "I'll talk to you tomorrow."

After Roberto left, Mario tried to stay awake, but he was exhausted and fell into the dream he had been waiting for. The river flowed slowly as he stood on the bank. His barrier of solitude had been rebuilt, the tires and trees piled higher than before. He stood there peacefully and watched the grove of cottonwoods across the water. Their thick green branches swayed above the greener mesquite. He was still the boy who built his first raft with his brother,

Francisco, but he was not going to be the boy whose father tore the small platform apart and threw it into the river. His father screamed at him never to build a raft again because he did not want his sons to be mistaken for "mojados." He said only "mojados" would think of building such a thing to get across, especially when the river was deep and they couldn't wade into America. Mario stood behind his wall of junk, crouched lower in the evening light of a peaceful and passable river and dreamed he came out from behind the barrier to wave to his father on the other side. He dreamed his father stopped hating the river, turning from the opposite bank instead. He pointed to let Mario know which direction to go to find the nearest bridge to his side. When he found the bridge, Mario joined his father in a dry crossing over water that did not need to be disturbed.

# THE GARDEN OF PADRE ANSELMO
a true story

Before her *padrino*, Don Benito, died, Leti went to church every Sunday with him. Her godfather made the painful effort, hobbling through the village to early morning mass. Leti was sixteen and the past two years she loved the old man who'd helped baptize her as a baby. Don Benito and Felipe, her father, had been brothers. After Felipe was killed by a robber two years ago, Don Benito spent as much time as he could with Leti. She was the one who had found her father in a pool of blood in the family grocery store.

In recent weeks Don Benito's health had deteriorated. When she appeared at his door an hour before the seven o'clock mass, the early light of the sun was outlining the village. He was waiting for her in his chair, dressed in his cheap black suit. Though his tiny house was only a few streets from the church, the walk took him nearly an hour. His face was gray with pain, and his back bent forward as he hobbled on his cane. The villagers were accustomed to seeing the young girl and her padrino coming slowly up the street. "Buenos días," they said, admiring the girl with the brown hair in the black *rebozo* that covered her head and shoulders.

That Sunday, as every Sunday, Padre Anselmo, the priest in Golondrina for twenty years, stood at the church door greeting his parishioners.

Aside from his clerical duties and his devotion to the church, Padre Anselmo was an excellent gardener. He transformed the rocky soil in the huge rear area of the church into a lush garden of trees, plants, and flowers. Every Sunday after mass, people visited the garden to admire and smell red and white roses, gardenias, chrysanthemums, lilac elders, willow trees, and other abundant shrubbery. Padre Anselmo set stepping-stones and benches in shady spots throughout the garden. The center of it, below the tallest willow, contained a stone shrine to San Antonio, patron saint of the poor. A three-foot statue of him was set in a semicircular grotto of polished marble. In front of the statue, a glass case on a small table of similar marble was placed to hold the *milagros*. These were tiny gold and copper medals and likenesses promised to San Antonio by worshippers in return for a miracle and an answered prayer. The glass case held gold hearts and statuettes of babies promised by mothers with sick children, arms and legs of copper promised by those with limb ailments. When cured or granted the favor, the person would bring the milagro and pray before the shrine, kneeling at the hard marble. The area around the shrine was covered with flowers, many of them brought by people and set before San Antonio, others cut by Padre Anselmo.

He was glad to see Leti and Don Benito this Sunday. Aware of the old man's illness, he wondered how the girl would handle his approaching death.

"Buenos días, Leticia," he said, smiling.

"Buenos días, Padre."

He bowed to Don Benito. "How are you feeling today, Don Benito?"

They shook hands, and the old man nodded, his shaggy hair blowing in the light breeze. "Fine, Padre. As long as you see me coming up the stairs, everything is fine."

After mass, when most of the congregation had left, Padre

Anselmo went into his garden and found Leti and Don Benito on one of the benches. They did not see him behind the rose bushes, but he was close enough to observe the pained expression on the girl's face.

"Your mother needs you at the store," Don Benito said.

Leti held his hand. "You need someone with you. San Antonio will make you better."

Don Benito smiled, then coughed. "All you can do is pray that San Antonio takes me peacefully."

It was the first time he'd mentioned death. His words sent chills through her body. She rose quickly and led him to the shrine of San Antonio, whom he prayed to several times a day. They knelt, made the sign of the cross, and prayed silently.

Padre Anselmo watched.

Three days later, Don Benito was confined to bed under the care of his neighbor, Doña Elena. The following Sunday, Leti went to mass alone. She felt lonely in the crowded sanctuary as she sat in one of the back rows. After the service, she went to the shrine for a brief prayer, then to the store to talk with her mother.

"There is nothing you can do for the poor man," her mother told her. They spoke in the storage room while Lupe waited on customers. Since her husband's death, Enedina had withdrawn into her own world of grief. She was curt with customers, waiting on them but refusing to socialize or accept their condolences.

"Don Benito has taken care of himself for years," she told Leti. "It is too bad he is sick, but there is nothing you can do. I want you here. Doña Elena is taking care of him. The fiesta is coming, and we need you."

Leti stared at her mother, wondering why she'd become so unfeeling. After her father's death, why had her mother not found strength in religion as she and her padrino had?

"I'm going to take care of him," Leti said.

Enedina shuffled cans on the shelves. "Go to church and pray for him," she ordered. "Then come back here and get to work."

Leti ran from the store. It was late evening, and the dirt streets were empty as Leti stepped through the mud puddles. It was her padrino's favorite time of the year, late July, when mighty thunderclouds rolled over the Sangre de Cristos. She came to the church on the way to Don Benito's house and decided to go through the garden. She would pray at the shrine of San Antonio.

In the damp evening air she smelled the flowers and green grass. She went through the gate in the black iron fence enclosing the garden and toward the shrine. As her eyes caught the dim blue of the marble grotto, she saw a yellow light reflecting off the glass case of milagros. She thought it was the evening sun, but when she drew closer, the light grew brighter as if flames were trapped inside. She stepped over rows of flowers, across a section that Padre Anselmo was preparing to plant, then made her way among the hanging willow branches. But then, as she approached the shrine, the light began to fade. She ran the last few yards and leaned over the case. The light vanished. She bowed and crossed herself before the statue of San Antonio. Two pots of fresh roses decorated the shrine. About to leave, she caught a shocking smell. Her nose burned with sharp, rancid fumes. None of the flowers or vegetation could be giving off such a powerful, searing odor. She gasped and ran from the garden toward her padrino's house. The smell faded as she ran. Had she looked back, she might have seen Padre Anselmo on the back steps of the rectory, watching her run.

She ran until she reached the plaza in the center of the village. Her padrino's house was in the alley across the way. She rested on a bench before going on, trying to catch her breath. She wiped her forehead with her scarf and felt her nose gingerly. All traces of the burning were gone. She wiped a tear from her eye, then stood and moved across the plaza. She had never encountered such a smell before. When it hit her, she'd thought the garden was going to burn.

Leti met Doña Elena coming out of her padrino's house. "Buenas noches," the woman said, smiling. She carried a basket with the remains of a meal. "Don Benito is asleep."

"Buenas noches," Leti replied. "How is he doing?"

"He ate the soup and some bread. He said to ask you to please come back in the morning. He's too tired to see anyone."

"I'll be here all day tomorrow," she told the woman.

Doña Elena placed a hand on Leti's shoulder. "We had a good talk. He wants to say so much to you. We prayed to San Antonio. Your padrino asked him to watch over you. The doctor is coming tomorrow. I'll check on him during the night."

"I want to stay." Leti moved toward the door.

"No, *mija*." The woman held her back. "There's nothing you can do by staying up all night with him. He's sleeping, and I'll be here tomorrow. Pray for him at home. Get some sleep. I'll be up early, and you can come by in the morning. We'll stay with him together until the doctor comes."

Leti walked through the dusk that fell over the red mountains and clothed the streets with changing light. When she got home, her mother and sister were still at the store. She lay wide awake in bed for several hours but turned off her lamp when she heard them arrive.

Early the next morning, as she reached the plaza, she saw Padre Anselmo and Dr. Ornedo talking in the doorway of her padrino's house. She ran across the plaza and to the house. Padre Anselmo reached for her, placing his hands on her shoulders.

"I'm sorry Leticia," he whispered. "Your padrino is dying."

Leti stared at the violet stole Padre Anselmo wore around his neck, the vest worn when blessing the dying.

"Is he dead?" she asked, her voice trembling.

Dr. Ornedo shook his head. Padre Anselmo prayed. Doña Elena emerged with tears in her eyes and embraced Leti. "I was going to get you," she said. "He wants to see you."

Leti arranged the scarf on her head and entered the musty room. Don Benito lay in his bed in one corner. Dozens of calendar photos, postcards, and pictures of San Antonio and Jesus Christ were pinned to the wall beside him. A sheet covered him to his shoulders. She knelt by the bed and held his hand. As she kissed him on the cheek, the old man's forehead quivered. He opened his eyes and tried to move his lips. He coughed and whispered, "I saw him, Leticia. I saw him."

"Who did you see, padrino?"

"San Antonio," the dying man rasped. "He takes care of us. My Leticia . . ."

The funeral mass and the burial were a blur of images to Leti. With her mind and body numb, all she remembered were her mother's arms around her, escorting her into the church. She didn't recall how many days it took, how quickly they buried him, what day it was finally over.

Leti stopped going to mass after Don Benito died, and refused to go near the church, least of all the garden. One night, as she lay in bed crying, she thought of her father and her padrino, both now gone, the faith they had encouraged in her also dead.

She began to work in the store regularly, growing distant from her mother and sister, obeying the orders they gave to sweep and mop the aisles before closing each night. Very little was said between them, though Leti saw her mother watching her silently throughout the day. One evening, while her mother and sister were taking a break and Leti was tending the store alone, Alfonso Gutierrez entered. He was sixteen like Leti and in the same class at her school, which was out for the summer. Her devotion to

Don Benito had been so complete that she rarely saw or spoke to other young people of the village. Alfonso had asked her to go with him to a couple of the fiestas, but she always refused.

Alfonso wandered through the rows of cans and past the bins of vegetables. Leti kept an eye on him from behind the counter. He was darker skinned than most boys and wore his long black hair in a tail. He picked a couple of apples from a basket and stepped to the counter.

"Hello, Leti." He smiled. "I haven't seen you in a long time."

Leti did not smile back. Acting businesslike, she took the apples and started to put them in a bag. "Will this be all?"

"Yes. I don't need a bag." He set coins on the counter and picked up the apples. He took a bite from one and looked admiringly at her. "We haven't seen each other in a long time," he repeated. "Would you like to go with me to the Kermez tomorrow night?"

She hesitated over this unexplained chance to do something different, perhaps lessen the thoughts of her padrino. "I would love to go to the Kermez," she answered, her heart pounding. It was easier to say yes than she thought. "What time?"

Alfonso choked on his bite of apple and almost spit it out, then recovered. "Oh, they're serving good food. We can eat there." He fidgeted with the apples, dropping one on the floor. He picked it up and retreated toward the door. "How about six?"

"Fine," Leti said as Alfonso stumbled out.

When her mother and sister returned to close the store, Leti did her chores quickly, then left to visit the cemetery for the first time since the funeral. At the cemetery gate Leti crossed herself, then entered. The evening sun spread orange beyond the cemetery hills. Shadows covered rows of gravestones. For a moment she forgot where Don Benito was buried, then went to the farthest row. Trembling, she knelt over the fresh grave marked with the small statue of San Antonio that Don Benito had wanted mounted on his grave.

Leti removed the pot of wilted flowers leaning against the marker. She reminded herself to bring fresh flowers next time. She broke into tears as she prayed a rosary over Don Benito. She managed one Our Father and two Hail Marys before she broke down and sobbed. Raising her head in anguish, she saw a woman placing flowers at a grave several rows away. The woman turned to look at the crying. Leti wiped her face and plucked a few blades of yellow grass from the plot. She spoke to the statue of San Antonio. "I will bring him flowers next time."

She started to pray the rosary again, but as she bowed her head, her nose was seared by the burning odor. The stench choked her, and she gagged. Covering her mouth, she ran toward the woman, who looked up and stopped her own prayers.

"Help me!" Leti pleaded, clutching her throat.

The woman stood. "What's wrong?"

"Don't you smell it?" Leti gasped between coughs.

"Smell what?"

The fumes spread through Leti's head. "That smell! Can't you smell it?" She choked and coughed.

"I don't smell anything." The woman backed away, as if Leti were crazy. "Are you okay? Where do you live?"

Leti ran, hurrying across the graves, then out the gate and down the hill, the smell receding as she gained distance from the cemetery.

Her mother noticed how ragged Leti's appearance was. When she reached home and entered the kitchen, she saw in her mother's eyes how terrible she looked. She dropped into a chair at the table. Enedina put the cover on a pot of beans.

"Where have you been? What happened to you?"

"I went to visit the cemetery."

Her mother shook her head. "Too soon. You're not ready." She turned back to the stove.

"Something happened there." Leti's voice quivered.

"What?"

"A terrible smell. It burned me."

Her mother came to the table. "What smell? They certainly don't leave the dead above ground."

"A smell I've smelled before. The day before he died."

Enedina placed her arms around Leti and ran a hand through her hair. "It is all right." She rested her head on Leti's. "I know you miss your padrino. It's going to be hard for a while."

Leti stood and they embraced. She couldn't remember the last time she'd been hugged by her mother. During the funeral, they'd held each other, but this was different. That night, as she lay in the dark, Leti prayed until she fell into a deep sleep.

The next evening, she told her mother about Alfonso and the Kermez. Enedina was surprised that her daughter had accepted a date.

Leti sat in her room on the edge of the bed, brushing her hair, getting ready. She couldn't decide between a blue scarf or a brown shawl with yellow fringe. She went to the small mirror for a final check. As she bent toward it, the burning smell hit her face.

She leaped back with a scream, and the smell disappeared. Enedina rushed into the room.

"Don't you smell it?" Leti pleaded.

"What is wrong with you? Get ready for the Kermez! Go to the Kermez!"

Leti calmed down and waited for Alfonso on the front porch. He was dressed in a white peasant shirt with matching baggy pants. Leti had never seen him so clean.

"You look pretty," he told her when she stepped off the porch.

"Thank you."

They strolled arm in arm toward the Kermez. It was an annual celebration in the village right before the summer harvest of the fields. Dozens of tables and booths were set in the empty lot next to the church. She always counted how many artists, farmers, and parishioners sold their crafts, vegetables, and many kinds of delicious food. The children played games and had piñata contests. People danced to the band of *conjunto* musicians.

Alfonso squeezed her hand. She felt nervous. They passed under red and green streamers and flags that fluttered on wooden posts. The grounds were packed with people. Children ran waving streamers and eating homemade candy. Vendors offered tamales, *cabrito*, *menudo*, and hot corn on the cob. Women in the booths cooked frantically in huge, black pots. A group of men dressed in costumes worn by their native ancestors danced in a circle in the middle of the crowd, bounding gracefully to the beat of four drums played by teenaged boys with animal masks on their heads.

Alfonso and Leti greeted several people, and he led her to a candy booth and bought her chocolate made from goat's milk. Alfonso took his turn at trying to crack a huge donkey piñata with a stick. Blindfolded, he missed every time. Padre Anselmo wandered among the people. It was the first time since the funeral that Leti had seen him.

She hoped he didn't know she was with Alfonso. "Hello, Leticia," he said. "Good to see you."

"Hello, Padre," she answered.

"I wish you would come to church. The Lord has not forgotten you and your padrino."

He placed a hand on her shoulder. "Please come see the new flowers I've planted in the garden. They are growing quite well."

"I will, Padre."

When Padre Anselmo left Leti, Alfonso took her to sit under

a cottonwood tree that towered over the grounds. "I'm going to get something to drink," he said. "Do you want anything?"

"I still have this." She held up her cup of lemonade.

She watched him join a group of boys beside one of the booths. She didn't like their looks. She hoped he wouldn't bring them back with him. After several minutes he returned alone and plopped down next to her with a grunt. He pulled a small flask from under his shirt and showed it to her.

"Where did you get that?" she asked.

"Roberto sold it to Juan and Tipi. They gave me some."

"That is going to get you drunk," she said. "Did you bring me here to drink?"

Alfonso shook his head and took a shot from the flask. He made a face and sighed. "Do you want some?" He held out the flask to her.

She smelled tequila on his breath and decided she had the courage. She took the flask and drank. She coughed. Alfonso laughed. She took a second shot and drew a deep breath as the warm liquid went down her throat. She smiled at Alfonso, then washed away the tequila taste with her lemonade.

He drew closer to her. "You are very nice," he whispered in her ear. He tried to lift her long skirt. She pushed his hand away. He hugged her with one arm and drank with the other. She nudged him away and sat up.

The fireworks display began with three bright explosions in the night sky. Leti accepted the flask from Alfonso and drank more. It was the first time she had drunk any alcohol, and she was amazed at how easy it was.

Suddenly, Alfonso laughed and pulled her closer. She swayed and fell on the cool grass. Alfonso rolled toward her and tried to plant a kiss on her mouth. Leti pushed him off and slapped him.

He laughed and slapped her in return. The shock made her roll away from him. She staggered to her feet.

"¡Cabrón!" She spit out the word as the world started to spin. She tried to straighten her skirt while Alfonso drank deeply from the flask. Then he reached for her leg. She jumped to one side, bent down, grabbed the flask, and hit him over the head with it. Alfonso laughed, then lay back, breathing heavily and giggling. She threw the flask on the ground beside him.

Leti swayed through the trees and away from the Kermez. She found the well at the end of the field and drew water using the wooden pail. She gargled and wanted to throw up. The well spun. Dizzy and angry, she leaned against the bricks and splashed water on her face. Suddenly, directly above the shimmering water in the pail, the burning fumes returned. They were more powerful than ever and seemed to rise from the earth through the well. The searing odor entered her nose and sobered her at once. The odor grabbed her throat, and she could not cry out.

"Dios, help me!" she gasped and ran.

Doña Elena answered the pounding at her door. Leti stood leaning against the wall beside it. "My child, what happened?" She guided Leti to her bed. "What's wrong?"

Leti lay back, sweat running down her face, her damp hair clinging to her neck.

Doña Elena brought water and a cloth and washed Leti's face. "Tell me what happened."

Leti related the incidents with the smell. When she finished, Doña Elena rose from the bed and knelt before a crucifix on the wall. She mumbled something and crossed herself, then returned to Leti.

"My child," she began. "I can tell you what the smell is."

"Have you smelled it?"

"No." She took Leti's hand. "But your padrino did. He told me about it the day before he died."

Leti stared at the crucifix on the wall. "My padrino smelled it?"

"Several times. San Antonio, as you know, was your padrino's favorite saint. He prayed often to him. When he was dying, he kept repeating that he could see San Antonio at the foot of his bed. And he told me that he could smell his tortured, burning feet and that it was a sign from God that his suffering would soon stop. Your padrino was not afraid. He said San Antonio, as the patron saint of the poor, helped many people during his life. He lived at the time of the Spanish Inquisition, when the rulers of Spain persecuted people they believed were against the Church. San Antonio was a brave man. One day, in helping a poor peasant who'd been whipped by soldiers, he was too defiant. The soldiers took him to prison. He was tried, found guilty of heresy, and sentenced to death."

Doña Elena's eyes widened. "The odor that you and your padrino smelled is the burning flesh of San Antonio. They tortured him by burning the soles of his feet, then finally killed him. The smell comes to a person when something important is going to happen. It is a message from our Lord and San Antonio. Your padrino told me he smelled it a few days before your father was killed. He said San Antonio appeared to warn him. You have smelled San Antonio for some special reason."

Leti and Doña Elena knelt before the crucifix and prayed. Then Leti left and crossed the plaza to the church and Padre Anselmo's garden. Fireworks exploded in the sky, balls of red and green raining down on the village. She passed the Kermez, which was more crowded than ever, and circled behind the church. As she entered the garden, the damp grass and freshly watered flowers moistened her face. She passed under the willow. The hanging branches slipped through her outstretched arms.

A light burned in the rectory window. As Leti knelt before San Antonio, a shadow crossed the window. She began to pray but was interrupted by a woman's cry at the gate. She turned. It was her mother. Leti rose and waved to her as fireworks showered more sparks on the cheering crowd.

"Leti! There you are!" She ran to her daughter as Alfonso staggered into view behind her. "He's drunk," Enedina said, out of breath. "He burst into the store like a loco, claiming you hit him and then disappeared." She grabbed Leti as they faced the reeling Alfonso.

Another rocket blossomed in the night. Leti stepped toward the raging Alfonso, covering her head with her scarf. He had a large bottle of tequila in one hand as he took a step into the garden. His drunken eyes had not yet found her in the darkness. A ball of light exploded in the sky and floated to earth, the crowd clapping for more. In the glare of the explosion, Alfonso saw Leti.

"¡Sangre de Cristo!" he cried, falling to his knees before her. He crossed himself, then rose swaying to his feet. His wild hair stuck to his face. His clothes were streaked with mud. Leti did not flinch.

"I only wanted to . . ." he began. "¡Madre de Dios!" He turned and ran into the night. Padre Anselmo appeared. Leti's mother ran to him, and the priest held her. The three of them looked up as more fireworks brightened the rows of freshly trimmed flowers.

## ACKNOWLEDGMENTS

The author thanks the editors of the following publications, where some of these stories first appeared: "The Jalapeño Contest," *Chelsea*; "Collecting Parrots," "Postcards," and "Spanish," *Flyway Literary Review*; "Spaceship," *LUNA*; "The Ghost of John Wayne," *Mirrors Beneath the Earth: Chicano Short Fiction* (Curbstone Press, 1992).

## ABOUT THE AUTHOR

Ray Gonzalez is a poet, essayist, and editor born in El Paso, Texas. He is the author of *Memory Fever* (The University of Arizona Press, 1999), a memoir about growing up in the Southwest, *Turtle Pictures* (The University of Arizona Press, 2000), which received the 2001 Minnesota Book Award for Poetry, and six other books of poetry, including *Cabato Sentora* (1999) and *The Heat of Arrivals* (1996), both from BOA Editions. The latter received a 1997 PEN/Oakland Josephine Miles Book Award for Excellence in Literature.

He is the editor of twelve anthologies, most recently *Muy Macho: Latino Men Confront Their Manhood* and *Touching the Fire: Fifteen Poets of the Latino Renaissance*, both from Anchor/Doubleday Books. He has served as Poetry Editor for *The Bloomsbury Review* for twenty years and recently founded a poetry journal, *LUNA*.

His awards include a 2000 Loft Literary Center Career Initiative Fellowship, a 1998 Fellowship in Poetry from The Illinois Arts Council, a 1993 Before Columbus Foundation American Book Award for Excellence in Editing, and a 1988 Colorado Governor's Award for Excellence in the Arts. He is an associate professor in the MFA Creative Writing Program at the University of Minnesota in Minneapolis.

# WORKS BY RAY GONZALEZ

ESSAYS AND MEMOIRS
*Memory Fever: A Journey Beyond* El Paso del Norte
*Turtle Pictures*

FICTION
*The Ghost of John Wayne and Other Stories*

POETRY
*Apprentice to Volcanos*
*Cabato Sentora*
*From the Restless Roots*
*The Heat of Arrivals*
*Railroad Face*
*Twilights and Chants*

ANTHOLOGIES
*After Aztlan: Latino Poets of the Nineties*
*City Kite on a Wire: 38 Denver Poets*
*Contemporary Poetry from Texas*
*Crossing the River: Poets of the Western U.S.*
*Currents from the Dancing River: Contemporary Latino Fiction,
    Nonfiction, and Poetry*
*Inheritance of Light*
*Mirrors Beneath the Earth: Short Fiction by Chicano Writers*
*Muy Macho: Latino Men Confront Their Manhood*

*Touching the Fire: Fifteen Poets of Today's Latino Renaissance*
*Tracks in the Snow: Essays by Colorado Poets*
*Under the Pomegranate Tree: The Best New Latino Erotica*
*Without Discovery: A Native Response to Columbus*

JOURNALS
*The Guadalupe Review*
*LUNA: A New Journal of Poetry*